BONE & ASH

Shadow & Ash Book 2

Isadora Brown

www.BOROUGHSPUBLISHINGGROUP.com

BONE & ASH
Copyright © 2022 Isadora Brown

ISBN: 978-1-957295-14-5

BONE & ASH

CHAPTER ONE

Hannah

Monsters live in the forest. Stay away. It leads to death.

My mother's hissed words echoed in my mind as I walked among silent trees and rustling branches. The Forest of Legend certainly deserved its description of being deep, dark, and ominous. For a moment, I thought I might be completely consumed by its bleakness.

Scraggly branches reached for me like bare arms hoping to snag at my dress. The thicket of leaves overhead blocked out the moon and the stars, preventing light from reaching down to guide me along the familiar path to the center of the woods. It was silent, as if even the animals had left, not wanting to run the risk of being one of the forest's victims.

In a way, my mother's urgent prophecy had been right. My best friend Claire Turner had succumbed to the forest. My heart clenched at the memory of her. It had been three moon cycles since the discovery of her body. To this day, no one knew the truth about what had truly happened to her, save for a select few. Patrol—even the self-righteous lieutenant Brendan Pickard—had lied about her cause of death, stating it as accidental. I'd been surprised about that, as they were usually sworn to tell the truth, no matter what.

The official story was a beast from the forest had mauled her during Consumption, on the night of Pyrate Mage Jonathan Nyx's attempted execution. I knew the truth. She'd been murdered by a Blood Beast, a creature that shouldn't exist.

I hated I couldn't remember the sound of her voice. She'd been gone for so long my memories of her were starting to fade, and no amount of magick I possessed was going to change that.

Behind me, a branch snapped, piercing the eerie stillness. I froze, waiting. My magick thrummed around me, circling my arms like a bracelet, and tingling my fingers. *You are protected*, it whispered.

My problem was I didn't know how to control it. Despite the research I'd done, I was still no clearer about how it all worked. It was why I'd once again reached out to the witch, Marcella, who dwelt in the forest. She was the one who would know about my magick, and help me master it.

I was surprised she'd agreed to meet with me again. In our last encounter, I'd taken a man called Sage Pascal with me. Part of the wealthy Pascal family, Sage was not as intimidating as his two older brothers, but he was still a Pascal, which meant he couldn't be trusted. This family had its own agenda and Marcella hadn't felt comfortable divulging anything with him nearby.

Nothing sinister emerged to reveal itself as the culprit of the snapped branch, so I forced myself to continue. Lingering in the forest was as dangerous as being here. I ducked, dodging a low branch, which still managed to pull at the back of my dress. Small, blunt leaves tangled themselves in my hair. I would have to remember to pull them out before I returned home or else the others would know I'd been gone. My feet continued to step over thick, gnarled tree roots. There were a couple of moments I tripped and almost landed flat on my face but managed to catch myself in time. I wished I could see in the dark.

No, you don't, my inner voice said. *Only beasts and Blood Mages can do that and you are not one of* them.

I swallowed down emotions at the thought of one particular infuriating Blood Mage. I hadn't thought of Adrian Blood in the months since I'd last seen him in my bedroom.

He ran the most profitable business on Ankura, catering to men, women, and monsters alike. His brothel allowed his clientele to purchase sexual favors with the people who worked there, especially the stolen women—Adrian would say reprieved— from their homes in Underedge. The Blood Mages feasted on these women, their only source of sustenance other than their usual supply of wild animals, a practice which had become boring to them. Yet they couldn't risk feeding on unsuspecting humans and being exposed. To Adrian, this compromise kept both Ankura and the Blood Mages safe.

I didn't agree. What about the women being fed upon—surely they didn't wish to be in the position they were in? Adrian had said it was a more humane way of ensuring innocents didn't get slain during a blood thirst, and he'd smiled, saying it was "only business." He'd posed a question—if there was no alternative for Blood Mages to feast, what would be the horrific consequences?

It didn't matter he was filtering them through a system he'd created, using assistance from other women such as my friend Claire and another woman named Anne—who was also dead. They'd both died because they were helping Adrian to do the right thing—in their opinion.

Even now, thinking about Adrian's part in all of this caused my stomach to churn and my cheeks to heat up. I abhorred the notion he could be okay with what I thought was such cruelty. I was reminded too of the Lost, people who also lived somewhere in this forest. Instead of being born, they'd been turned, which meant they were hungrier, more animalistic, and more dangerous.

I wondered if all Blood Mages would revert to that if they could not feed on living flesh. I suppressed a shudder and cast all thoughts of Adrian away. *This* was why I didn't wish to waste my time thinking of him. I could never figure out if I was disgusted or awed by him. He confused me and I didn't like the conflicting feelings raging inside of me.

I continued through the forest and then stepped into the same glade from before, surrounded by trees, forming the shape of a circle. I saw no one else waiting, and brought my trembling fingers to my mouth, thinking of how alone I was at present. If something attacked me, there was no one around to help me.

Again, my mother's voice tinkled in my ear, telling me I shouldn't be here, to stay away from the forest because monsters lived here. I was old enough now to know the truth. Monsters lived everywhere. They owned brothels and accumulated wealth through the buying and selling of people. They slaughtered and thieved and feasted on innocence.

Monsters weren't only found in spooky forests, and perhaps one of them was out there right now. I reached for my magick again, knowing that while I didn't wish to expose my secret to any potential attacker, I would if it meant saving my life.

"I can hear your heartbeat from across the forest, Hannah Walker."

The familiar voice slid down my back and coiled around my skin like a snake. I blinked, trying to locate it. I recognized it as Marcella's—she had a long, low drawl, difficult to forget— but I wasn't sure if that made me more fearful or less. At least I was no longer alone, though Marcella was not someone I could trust. I didn't know her. Not really.

"Your heartbeat reminds me of a little bird's," she continued. "Right before a hunter strikes it with his arrow."

I stopped, whipping around to see behind me, wincing as my neck muscles protested. I still couldn't see her. I was a mouse trapped in the corner of a manor by a house cat. Except the cat was toying with me, waiting until I slipped up before putting me out of my misery.

Her laughter tinkled all around me. I felt fire and ice on my skin, and turned back again, hair snapping from my braid and falling over my shoulder. I stumbled forward and bent at the waist, trying to catch my balance and almost failing. My heart pounded against my chest like an ancient war drum the enchantresses used to beat during the Magickal War. The darkness was a mask, suffocating me, making it more and more difficult to breathe. My face was on fire, and I believed I'd combust and the breeze would spread my ashes across the forest.

"Why are you so fearful?" Her voice echoed quietly and precisely right behind me.

I shrieked and snapped around, my skirts flying in a parody of swirling dance. There she was, at my shoulder, standing there as if she had been there the entire time. Maybe she had. Or perhaps she was only a vision, tricking me. An enchantment placed by the forest.

I squeezed my eyes shut, pinching the bridge of my nose and furrowing my brow.

When I opened my eyes, she was still there.

Marcella was not tall. Her brown hair fell like flat string, and her smooth, light brown skin glowed in the darkness. How that was possible considering the trees blotted out the moon, I didn't know. She wore a simple, bold-colored dress, much like the one I wore. It was fuchsia. I could make that out clearly, despite the lack of light.

Freckles danced on her cheeks and the bridge of her nose, and her dark eyes, outlined in kohl, were fixed on me. Her red lips curved up into a smirk. "Well?" She arched a brow. "Why are you so afraid?"

"I...why wouldn't I be?" I asked. My lips quivered, causing my words to be barely decipherable. I thrust my shaking hands behind my back, trying to get a hold of myself.

Marcella's eyes dropped to the back of her left hand and she flexed her fingers. She fiddled with a ring placed on her middle finger. "Are you afraid of *me*?"

"A little," I admitted. "And we *are* in the Forest of Legend."

"And?" Marcella didn't even look at me as she continued to adjust the piece of jewelry. "Who says the forest is a bad place to be? Witches live here, in their coven. If the forest was so bad, do you think we would choose to be here?"

"My mother warned me of this place," I said. "She said monsters live here. She said to stay away."

"Perhaps you and your mother have different opinions of what a monster is," Marcella said. She dropped her hands to her sides.

"Why did you wish to meet with me? Is it about your magick…or a certain Blood Mage?"

My face wrinkled at the mention of Adrian Blood. "Why would I meet with you about him?" I asked.

"Because your unresolved feelings are obvious," Marcella said. "Anyway, since you came naught for him, perhaps I should warn you. He will seek you out, and soon."

My heart skipped a beat. Adrian would seek me out? I thought back to the last time I saw him, the possessive glint in his eye. I remembered tasting his blood, remembered wanting more of it. Even now, my mouth salivated at the thought.

Another snapped twig, and then someone muttered.

Marcella's lips formed a thin line. "Sage Pascal," she said. "For a little thing, you have the courage of a lion."

Before I realized what was happening, Sage Pascal emerged from the thicket of trees. So he had been the one following me. I'd thought it was my overactive imagination. The forest wasn't conducive to rationality.

Sage was handsome, with golden-brown hair and pale green eyes. Being a Dwarf, he stood to my waist, but the way he walked with such confidence, he commanded attention in the same way his two six-foot-plus older brothers might have. Even though he crept through the forest like a wraith still he was adorned in the finest silks, revealing his wealth. He didn't even look sheepish as he joined us in the middle of the awning.

"Why am I not surprised to find you here?" I asked him, narrowing my eyes.

"Considering I stated I'm conducting my investigation on what happened to your friend, I'd say you shouldn't be surprised at all," Sage said. "Despite Patrol closing the case and labeling it as accidental, I have a feeling they might be wrong."

"So, you decided to follow me?" I asked, not bothering to hide my annoyance. I put my hands on my hips and leaned forward slightly.

"You're the one with the magick, and the friend who lives in the scary forest, and ties to a real Blood Mage," Sage pointed out, "So, yes, you would be the ideal one to follow."

I rolled my eyes and turned to Marcella. "Why are you okay with him being here?" I realized who I was speaking to and took a step back. I didn't wish to talk to her thusly. I didn't want her turning me into a toad—or worse—with her magick.

"Don't assume because I speak freely in front of him, I'm satisfied with him," Marcella said. "However, for a Pascal, this one has a good heart, even if it is a miniature one. Compared to his brothers, it is the heart of a lion." She took a step toward me. "It is necessary for you to learn your magick, child. You come to me, seeking answers, answers I can't give. But I assure you, you have all the knowledge you need to know here," she placed her fingers to her brow, "and here." She dropped her fingers to her chest. "You must trust yourself and accept what you are to establish control over yourself. If you can't do either, you'll fail."

"But how do I—"

"You must look inside yourself to find the answer," Marcella said. "I can't give it to you, nor can anyone else. I know you came to me because you believe I can train you to know your magick the way you know yourself. But I can't."

My chest grew tight. If Marcella couldn't help me, who could? I had no one left to turn to.

"But *you* can," Marcella said. "It is your magick, a part of you, just as your eyes and your legs are. You know what to do with those. Befriend your magick, accept the shadows and the light, and I promise you, you will control it."

I opened my mouth to retort, but she held up a hand. "Go. I've said all I want to say on the matter. Mark my words, Hannah Walker—no one can train you the same way you can train yourself. And if your powers want to, you must ask what they want from you in return. Nothing is ever for free." With those last, chilling words, she disappeared.

"Well, then," Sage said, speaking in the silence. "That answered nothing." He offered me his arm. "Shall we?"

I pulled my gaze from where Marcella had been and made my way toward Sage. As the two of us began to make the trek back to the manor, I couldn't help but wonder how to start training myself. She seemed to think I could figure it out. There was a small part of me concerned that, despite her faith in me, I'd be unable to do so.

CHAPTER TWO

Hannah

By the time we returned to the manor, I was exhausted. Sage and I parted ways. As annoying as he was, I'd been glad of his company— it had made the darkness more bearable. I got into my room and saw a silhouette in the middle of the floor.

"Han?" Lizzie's voice filled the silence of my room and I nearly wept with relief. If it had been my father or Diego Pascal, I wasn't sure what I would have done, or what excuse I would have used for my night excursion.

I need to get better at lying.

A flicker of candlelight sliced through the darkness as she approached, her shadow outlined on the wall.

"What are you doing out so late?" she asked, head cocked to the side, eyes narrowed. She blinked once. "You aren't meeting with —"

"I'm not," I said, brushing past her, almost catching the sleeve of my dress on the small candle flame. My limbs screamed in exhaustion. "I haven't seen him in months, Lizzie." I stopped in front of my wardrobe and pulled it open, looking for a nightgown. I paused, glancing over my shoulder at her. "Read me, if you don't take my word for it."

Lizzie flinched at my words, and part of me was glad for it. I received no joy in hurting her with a petty comment, but I didn't appreciate the fact that she'd broken the unspoken rule not to use our magick on each other before. Since then, it was difficult to trust her.

"No, it's just…" Her voice trailed off, and she clutched a hand to her chest, as though she wanted to calm her racing heart. "I wanted to make sure you were safe." She glanced around the room. I couldn't be sure, but her face was pale. It worried me. My older sister didn't get scared too easily. Something had spooked her…but what?

"Ankura is getting more and more dangerous."

I returned my attention to the wardrobe, going through the various nightgowns I owned. "Oh?" I asked, trying to keep the tremor from my voice. "What makes you say that?"

"I've heard the whispering," she said. She took a couple of steps to my window but stopped before she reached it. "More and more people are coming into my shop to purchase weapons. They're scared."

"Fear doesn't mean something bad is happening," I said.

I settled on a white nightgown and pulled it out. I hoped Lizzie didn't notice my shaking fingers. I was trying to keep myself rooted in reality, but all this discussion of a possible war between Underedge and Ankura made me think of Adrian and what he was doing. I didn't want to worry about him, but I couldn't help it.

"Yes, I know that," Lizzie said. She tucked a stray curl of hair behind her ear and pulled her gaze from the window. "I still think we should be ready, in case."

She brushed by me again, this time to set the candle down on my nightstand, and returned to stand behind me. She began to unlace my corset, her fingers strong and nimble.

"What do you mean?" I asked. I couldn't look at her over my shoulder so I kept my gaze on her shadow on my wall. "Lizzie, you know something. What is it?"

Lizzie was silent for a moment. When she finished her task, she took a step back. I eased my arms out of their sleeves and stepped out of the dress before picking up the nightgown.

I threw it over my head and once it covered me, I straightened out the skirts, picked up my discarded dress, and tossed it into a basket already filled with soiled clothing. Roseanna, my lady in waiting, would pick it up in the morning, and it would all be washed in the next couple of days.

"Lizzie," I tried again, turning to face her. I needed her to trust me with her knowledge, with whatever it was.

"I've been using my gift, Han," Lizzie said. Closer now, her skin was sallow and her eyes were burnt ash. It was strange not to see them vivid, lively. Even at her darkest moment, she always had a spark in her irises that made her distinctly Lizzie. But now...

"I thought you were against using your gift," I said, "especially on the unsuspecting. What if you were discovered?" My ire began to rise and I stomped over to her. The candle flickered as I brushed past, the air surrounding me causing it to dance. "I know you to be reckless, Lizzie, but not stupid."

"Aunt Thaya suggested I do it," she said, an edge to her voice.

I stopped completely. "You've been seeing Aunt Thaya?" I asked. Thaya was my mother's sister and a known witch.

Lizzie nodded, bringing her hands to her lap. She began to pick at her nails.

"Now that the Pascals are here, Diego is engaged to Everly, and you have some sort of relationship with Adrian Blood, I...I wanted to protect myself," she said. "Protect you, Everly, and my family, if I must."

I opened my mouth, then shut it. My stomach twisted with something, an emotion I couldn't name. I wasn't sure if I supported her actions. I was disappointed she'd not told me until now, and I was curious what Aunt Thaya could do that would make her feel empowered enough where she felt confident, even with the rumors swirling around.

I also didn't know how to respond to Lizzie's assumption that Adrian Blood and I were in any sort of relationship. My stomach churned with disgust. I felt emotions for Adrian before I knew what he truly was...even afterwards if I was being honest. Feelings I refused to analyze, refused to even speak about, even to myself.

"You should come with me tomorrow to see Thaya," Lizzie said after a long moment.

I arched a brow. "Me?" I pursed my lips as a cool breeze tickled my exposed back.

Lizzie noticed my shudder and began to lace up my gown. "Yes," she said. "Our magick may not be the same, but I'm certain Thaya could help you as she's helped me."

"How has she helped?" I asked, trying to turn my head so I could glance at her over my shoulder.

"She's taught me how to control my magick," Lizzie said.

I froze. "She…she what?" This time, I did turn around. My magick tingled. I didn't want to use my magick on Lizzie. Just because she had didn't mean I needed to let her behavior dictate my own, but for the briefest of moments, I was tempted to see if she was lying.

Marcella's words flitted through my mind. I tried to keep my face blank. As much as I wanted to trust Lizzie, I didn't. She could penetrate my mind with magick and steal away any thoughts and secrets I didn't wish her to discover. I didn't want her to know I'd met with Marcella tonight.

"Do you think she'd have me?" I asked. I didn't know much of Thaya, other than she lived in the Forest of Legend with her coven. Since Patrol tended to keep out of the forest, she and her coven were free to do magick because no one was brave enough to stop it.

"I'm sure of it," Lizzie said. "I'm sure she'd want the Becketts too. Our cousins all possess some form of magick, you know. We inherited it from our mothers. At least, that's what Thaya told me, and considering she's a High Priestess within her coven, I believe her. Though, since our mother and their mother disappeared, Thaya feels obligated to teach us what they can't: who we really are."

I considered the idea. Maybe Thaya would be able to help, especially since she was my aunt and might know more about me better than anyone else. Especially since Marcella had rejected me.

"Will you come?" Lizzie asked. She stepped around me once she finished helping me with the dress and took my hands in hers. Her golden eyes caught mine, and there was such fierce intensity in the hazel orbs I flinched. "Please say you will, Han. There is so much I want to tell you but can't."

I frowned. "What can't you tell me?" I asked. "Surely you know you can trust me."

"Yes, of course," Lizzie said quickly, "but the coven has its rules. I can't betray them, even to you."

I didn't want to admit her words hurt me, but they did. It felt as though there were two sides and she had picked someone else's.

"But," Lizzie said, taking my hand in hers. "I want to tell you everything, Han. I do. It all makes sense now. We're descended from this ancient magickal line—did you know magick is inherited through the mother's line? It makes sense, but still. So, when we have children, if we do, they'll inherit our magick from us."

I sighed, my brain racing. After Marcella and now this, I needed a moment alone to let this settle.

"But there's more to it than that," Lizzie continued. She dropped my hand and began to pace with more enthusiasm than I realized could be possible so early in the morning. "There's so much more to it, Hannah. I want to share it all with you. I hope to. Will you come?"

"When?" My eyelids were at half-mast and I proceeded to crawl into bed. Hopefully, Lizzie would take the hint and understand I longed for sleep.

Lizzie chuckled. "Does training with Aunt Thaya bore you so?" she asked. "I said, will you come with me? I can take you as early as tomorrow afternoon. Though, I suppose technically that would be later today."

"Yes." My eyes locked with hers and I moved the covers as I was almost smothered in them. At least afternoon time meant I didn't have to step into the Forest of Legend in the dark. Perhaps it wouldn't be as terrifying during the day, though I wasn't quite convinced. "Yes, I will come."

"Good," Lizzie said. Her lips turned up in a small smile. "I'm glad." She grabbed the candle from the nightstand and began to make her way to the door. By the time she got there, there seemed to be a skip to her step, liveliness that hadn't been there before. "Good night, sister."

"Good night."

Left alone in the darkness, my thoughts turned back to the night of Jonathan Nyx's planned execution, when someone had pulled my magick from me and used it to help him escape his fate. Since that night, I'd not been able to access my powers in the same manner.

No, that's not true, my inner voice pointed out, distorting my thoughts. *You accessed your magick when you saved Adrian from Pepper.*

I banished the thought from my mind. I didn't want to think about Adrian. Although, perhaps I could figure out how to access my magick without Aunt Thaya. Should I take Marcella's advice and do this on my own? But what if I failed? If war *was* coming, I needed to be informed on how to access and use my magick as fast as possible. I didn't have the luxury of time. Aunt Thaya was family so surely she would not manipulate me or my magick. I'd need to take a risk and hopefully keep things in the family.

CHAPTER THREE

Adrian

Humans who believed in their Five Gods took the first day of the week as one of rest. It meant today I'd receive no customers for my brothel—besides Blood Mages who didn't believe in such religious trivialities. Ankura was quiet. Peace surrounded the small port town on days like today, where businesses closed up and humans went to their temples and worshipped gods with no tangible proof they even existed.

I took advantage of the lack of brothel business to perform some of my more dubious tasks. Time to collect my delivery. The first day of the week was when I had my pickup at the eastern shoreline, at the docks on the other side of Ankura.

Despite the island's small size, the population tended to live in the west. The majority of the island was filled with vegetation and jungle, not including the forest, and only the damned felt safe traveling through such precarious areas.

No one explored the island, which meant I could use it to transport the women I acquired from Underedge as part of the deal between Ankura and Underedge. This deal kept Blood Mages fed without loss of other's life, and our existence hidden. My ladies provided the only source of living food that wasn't animal. Feasting on them was less than ideal since they tasted of salt water and brine, but it was a better option than feasting on the cows and the pigs that made up the few farms on the island. Even if we did that, the farmers would notice and suspicion would arise. And the lack of human blood would certainly take its toll on the Blood Mages and then what? They'd feast on anyone with a pulse.

My way, no one noticed the women, the Sirens. No one seemed to care who they were or where they came from. They were a meal, a consensual sexual pleasure. That was it.

I had to travel through the Forest of Legend to get where I needed. It was the fastest route—directly across the forest—and I couldn't be seen by curious, prying eyes. I also had the cover of darkness to help me. The Dark Moon always caused me to be more on edge than I liked. I knew the witches saw it as a new start, so to speak, throwing wishes at the darkness like children threw scraps of parchment in bottles and tossed them into the ocean. The sky being so inky black always left me…unsettled.

I knew the forest so I could rush through without needing to be wary of anything unexpected. It was how I got from the abandoned docks, where my ship was, to the brothel. My ship was as vulnerable and as precious as my heart or my throat; if a human destroyed it with fire while I was in slumber, there would be no way for me to stop it. I would perish with it, turning into nothing but ash.

Thaya and her coven of witches were performing some ceremony tonight so I was keen to avoid them. Blood Mages and witches were not always on best terms, and while I didn't mind pushing her occasionally to see how she might react, I was in no mood to do so now.

Especially now I knew she was Hannah's aunt.

There was something about her tie to Hannah I didn't wish to explore. I hoped Hannah never sought out information regarding her magick from the woman. The coven was filled with selfish individuals who wanted to take magick and use it for their purposes. While I was unaware what those purposes were, I didn't think they were good. Thaya and Hannah might be blood, but I didn't trust Thaya once she found out the truth about Hannah's powers, if she didn't know already.

And why do I care? I refused to acknowledge the question.

I slid around a tree, shrouded in nothing but darkness. Not even the stars sparkled in the sky, as though they refused to do so without some glimmer of the steady moon. There was no low thrum of animal noises, no croaking toads or buzzing insects, no squawking birds or hooting owls. It was silent, which should be enough to deem this place as eerie as it seemed. Hannah Walker knew more about me than most people, thanks to Pepper deciding to share that information with her. Hannah was someone I trusted. As much as she loathed me, loathed what I was and what I represented, I knew she'd never harm me.

A strange feeling of warmth enveloped the inside of my body. I shook it off. I didn't want to feel…that. Whatever the hell *it* was. I stepped around another tree and ducked my head, dodging a high branch. I plucked a fallen leaf from my hair, dropping it to the floor before smoothing the locks back into place.

I stepped out of the forest and made my way to the docks. My feet echoed against the rotting wood of the planks making up the boardwalk. I considered for a moment employing a witch to fix them and have it so my footsteps were silent, but that would risk someone else knowing about my movements. Of course, I could kill her afterwards, and feast on her blood, if I chose to. Other Blood Mages would. But I wasn't one of them.

After Claire's murder, we didn't need any more untimely deaths. With Brendan Pickard lieutenant of Ankura's section of Patrol, it would guarantee *some* sort of investigation.

Since he'd been forced to close Claire's case and label it as accidental, I was sure he'd try to seek out the truth and ensure he never again had to do anything that went against his pathetic morals.

No, better to hear my footsteps than invite trouble.

As I'd expected, Black Shore was empty by the time I reached it. Because of how close it was to the forest, and there was no way to reach the shore unless one traveled through the forest, it was never used. As such, the white sand remained untouched, as did the docks themselves, which were filled with mold and creaked under even the weight of a bird. One spot on the docks was caved in so no one could step on it without risking falling through to the ocean.

I was a regular visitor and had been here once a week. I knew where to step, where to avoid, and where to wait. I didn't like to wait, and normally, I didn't have to. The usual lackey working for Underedge as a delivery boy knew I expected him to be on time and wouldn't tolerate tardiness.

Tonight, however, he wasn't here when I expected him.

I cast my gaze to the ocean. The waves were weak against the Black Shore. Even during torrential storms, this part of the ocean was protected by the shape of the island and where it was positioned. I couldn't see any hint of anyone coming to drop off several Sirens. There was no dip in the ocean, no foam bubbling to the surface before they emerged from the depths. Besides the gentle lapping of the ocean as it licked the shore, the night was silent.

This couldn't be a good sign. I continued to wait. The boy had never been this late before. He knew I had better things to do than to wait around for him.

For a moment, I considered perhaps I had my dates jumbled up, and today wasn't our normal meeting time. Since Pepper had been killed, betraying me, it was taking more time than I would have cared to admit getting the brothel back under proper management. I couldn't trust anyone to do it the way I had so foolishly trusted her to, which meant I was shouldering it all.

I didn't like having to manage when the bartenders should come in, and which girl had an evening off because of health reasons. I wasn't fond of speaking with the girls, especially Hessie. Despite her position within the brothel as one of the more requested Sirens, she walked around with an air of entitlement.

Nowadays the days bled together as I was forced to do the grunt work. I barely even interacted with Reginald Walker when he collected my dues and didn't notice when Hannah wasn't with him.

That was a lie. I always noted her absence. I hated I noticed it at all.

I thought of the last moment we were together, the way I kissed her neck. The way she let me. She tasted delicious, of something sweet with just a touch of salt. I could only imagine what her blood might taste like.

But no. I banished the thought. Thinking of her in that way, especially right now when I should be focused on the task at hand, could distract me, and any distraction right now could be lethal.

I fixed my eyes on the ocean. The water was still silent and smooth. It looked as though I could walk on the surface if I wanted to.

I glanced up at the black sky. As it was too dark, I couldn't do the usual and tell the time by looking at the position of the moon in the sky. I had no way to observe the passage of time, and I didn't like it.

Without warning, the ocean dipped. Water started pulling back from the shore by an unknown force. Something was coming.

Finally.

I took a step back, then two. The water continued to recede until a familiar silhouette emerged. He was a merman, wearing the royal Underedge insignia—a trusted soldier for the underwater kingdom. He walked awkwardly, still unsteady on his feet, despite the fact he'd done this once every month for the past year. I watched him walk over to me, though I couldn't help but notice he was alone.

Where are my ladies?

I scowled and glanced behind him. Surely, he hadn't come to me empty-handed? He couldn't be this stupid. By the time he stood in front of me, salt water dropped from his body, and he pushed back long brown locks that clung to his face behind his ear. He said nothing, dropping his hands to his hips.

"Well?" I barked out. "Where is the week's delivery?"

I was expecting two women—I was going to remove a couple from the brothel, but I needed to replace them with the new ladies before I could let them go—or the remaining Sirens would be overworked and overused.

The boy looked down. He picked up his bare foot and began to dig into the sand with his toe. He couldn't be much older than sixteen, perhaps seventeen. He reminded me of Hannah, but Hannah had eyes that could have been around for centuries. This merman was green—a fresh new face with inexperience.

"I have no delivery for you," the boy said. He still wouldn't look at me.

I went still, letting the words sink in. Surely I hadn't heard him correctly, not when he was standing in front of me, mumbling from the corner of his mouth? I didn't know what to say to that, knowing I would lose my temper in mere seconds if I didn't get a handle on myself.

"What does that mean?" I asked, each word punctuated with a warning. I put my hands behind my back and grasped my wrists. I needed something to sink my fingers in as my fury began to tease my insides.

"It means, I have no delivery for you," the boy said again. There was a hint of confusion to his voice, as though he didn't know any other way to explain the circumstance to me.

"Why not?" I demanded.

"I-I-I-" He took a step back, then another. I didn't realize I had moved to follow him until the tips of my booted feet were standing in the ocean. The water couldn't soak my feet, but it pressed into the leather of the boots and caused a chill to linger on my spine.

"Spit it out, boy," I said, leaning toward him. I didn't care if he took this as some sort of threat. I needed answers. I needed the new women to be able to free two older ones. "I will not have you waste my time with your drivel."

"I went to retrieve the two Sirens for our scheduled delivery," the boy said. "But they weren't there. I waited and waited. It's why I'm late."

"And?"

"And they never came," the boy said. "The shipment never arrived."

I pressed my lips together. There was much I wanted to say, but I held back. "Why are you here?" I asked after a moment. "What makes you come to me if you have nothing to give me?"

"I-I...I didn't want you telling Mr. Pascal I had failed," he admitted. "I swear I was at my post on time. But no one came. I thought telling you, you might be able to figure out what happened."

"You are certain the delivery wasn't late?" I asked.

He locked eyes with me. "It has never been late, and I don't think it's late now," he said.

"What are you telling me?" I asked.

"The Sirens are gone," the boy said. "I think...I think someone found out what we're doing and took them."

CHAPTER FOUR

Hannah

As I followed Lizzie through the forest, I shook off the feeling someone was watching us from the trees. The sun had long since set. The last few times Lizzie had come here was during the day, but perhaps my presence forced her to take extra precautions. Or perhaps she didn't trust me with the coven's location yet.

I continued to follow her through the maze of thick trunks and bark. I hiked up my skirt, careful not to trip over any of the gnarled, thick roots jutting out of the dirt. Lizzie seemed to glide through the forest without any qualms. Either she didn't believe in the stories or they didn't scare her. Part of me envied her confidence. I wished I had the means to bottle it and use it whenever I had the chance. As it was, I could only fake it, and I wasn't adept at doing even that.

"Are we almost there?" I asked in a low whisper. I ducked my head, my chin nearly clipped by a low-hanging branch.

"It's just a few paces ahead," Lizzie said. She glanced over her shoulder, and even through the pure darkness, a smile tilted her lips up. "You aren't telling me you still believe in Mother's ghost stories, are you?"

I opened my mouth to respond to her, but then shut it. Instead of responding to the teasing look on my sister's face, I dropped my gaze to the ground.

"I am only teasing, sister," Lizzie said. She took my hand within hers and gave it a gentle squeeze, turning her attention forward. "The forest is not so scary, once you get used to it."

"What?" I yelped. I looked around, afraid I had woken up some sleeping beastie who was going to swallow us whole. I lowered my voice, leaning forward. "How can you say that? Lizzie, the stories aren't all false. Monsters do live here."

"Pray tell, have you seen one yourself?" Lizzie asked. She skirted around a branch so quickly, I had no time to move. Instead, it poked at my arm as I hissed in pain.

"Well, Han? You've been here a couple of times, are you telling me you've witnessed these monsters with your own eyes?"

"Blood Mages—"

"Don't exist," Lizzie said firmly.

I wanted to lean into my magick, to see if she believed that, but I didn't. Instead, I inhaled deeply. The scent of smoke tingled my nostrils, and I stifled a sneeze. I closed my eyes, recognizing the strong and leafy scent.

It wasn't only smoke. It was sage.

This time, it had nothing to do with any Pascal family member and everything to do with the forest and magick. When sage was used, it was said to vanquish negative energy and clear out unwanted spirits. It was also a cleansing tool. Mother used sage after arguments she and Father got into, as though she was freeing the house of the negative energy the two of them created. I'd been surprised Father indulged her; the ritual itself was filled with witchiness, but he didn't seem to mind.

My father would have done anything for her because he'd adored her. My heart squeezed at the thought. That was a memory I hadn't thought of in a long while.

Shaking off the sudden sadness, I continued to follow Lizzie, now a few paces in front of me. If I moved quickly, I might be able to catch up—

In my haste, I didn't see a twisted root, and I tripped over it. I managed to throw out my hands at the last moment to catch my fall. My hands screamed in pain as they hit the ground, and Lizzie stopped, turning around.

"Hannah?" she asked when she saw me picking myself up. "What are you doing back there? Don't dally. Thaya isn't one for tardiness."

I blew out a breath, wiping my hands on the skirt of my dress. I wasn't one for tardiness either but attempting to rush through this forest was impossible.

After what seemed like another hour, Lizzie stopped. I nearly ran into her back but managed to plant my feet on the ground and maintain control of my center before I collided with her.

I blew out a breath, and then another. My heart fired rapid beats against my chest. I was unsure where to put my hands, so I dropped them to my sides and wiped them nervously on my skirts.

"Why are you so frightened, Hannah?" a voice asked from behind me.

Another person asking me that. Were they not aware this forest was deadly?

I jumped out of my skin, whirling around to find Aunt Thaya there, tilting her head up to catch my gaze. She came up to my chin, but still had this power of stepping into a place and commanding attention. Her golden-hazel eyes locked on me as though she could bring my deepest, darkest secrets to the surface with her pointed gaze. Her golden hair ran up and down her back; bangs danced across her visage, highlighting her oval-shaped face, and she wore a dress more revealing than any I had seen before.

I couldn't stop the flush as it crept up my skin and tickled the tips of my cheeks. The dress itself was sleeveless, dipping low in front of Thaya's chest. She wore no corset, so it revealed more skin than I had seen before outside of artwork. It clung to her like a second skin, hugging her waist before dropping in different lengths to flutter around her thighs, her legs. She wore nothing on her feet save for a beaded bracelet around her ankle and rings that adorned different toes.

"My dear niece," Thaya said. "I've been expecting you." A soft smile on her face caused a dimple to pop in her left cheek. She took my hands in hers and gave them a gentle squeeze. "I'm so glad you are here. There is much to tell you."

***

Thaya didn't tell me much new in truth, as most of it I'd already gathered myself. Magick was distributed to children from the mother's line. Lizzie had said as much. Some inherited, some didn't. Magick manifested on the brink of adulthood—for girls, around eleven or twelve, while boys didn't manifest until thirteen or fourteen.

What I wasn't aware of was the fact that my mother and my two aunts were descended from Eve, the first witch to be burned alive at the stake.

The reason for the first Consumption.

It reminded me of the last one Ankura was supposed to have, before someone pulled my magick from me and helped Pyrate Mage Jonathan Nyx escape. It was not the first time the pyrate escaped from his death, and I doubted it would be the last.

Except now, Diego Pascal was after him.

To get my uncle, the governor of Ankura, to allow his youngest daughter, Everly, to be betrothed to him, Diego had to promise my uncle the head of Jonathan Nyx. An impossible task, to be sure, but somehow, he managed to convince my uncle because the two had been engaged the past two months, much to Everly's displeasure.

"Eve's death is why most of our family are fire witches," Thaya explained.

I wasn't sure what I was, but I knew I was no fire witch. The magick I used was light. It wasn't fire, unless the two were related in some way.

I looked over at Lizzie. "You're…?"

"I am," she said with a nod, her lips curving up almost shyly. It was difficult for me to associate Lizzie and the word "shy" together at all, but the way she looked when Thaya was around, it wasn't the abrasive Lizzie I was used to. She almost seemed…docile, as though she was ready to take instruction.

"Do you know what you are?" Thaya asked me. Her voice was curious, but there was also a sense of knowing, like she had her guess but was curious about what I thought. It was as though the knowledge itself wasn't important, but my perception of it was.

I opened my mouth, then shut it. I didn't know if answering her was the best thing to do. I didn't like that instinctively I didn't trust her. This was my aunt, my mother's sister. She might have an alternative lifestyle frowned upon by society and should Patrol ever catch them doing magick there was a good chance they could lose their life over it, but I couldn't feel comfortable talking to her about my magick. And I didn't think it had anything to do with Lizzie being present.

"I'm not sure what I am," I admitted. "I suppose that is why I'm here, to garner answers for myself."

Thaya gave me another look. I held my breath. Was she able to tell if I was lying or not? Did her magick allow her the same ability that I, myself, possessed? Perhaps I should have thought of that before I answered her.

After another moment, her lips curled up and she smiled. "Of course," she said. "Lizzie, too, was ignorant. We want to help you find yourself, and your true nature. I'm glad you came to us. I'm glad you trust us."

Trust. I didn't trust her. But I couldn't tell her that.

Instead, I let her place her hand on the small of my back and lead me toward another thicket of trees. The crunch of the ground behind me told me Lizzie was following me.

The trees were less gnarled and intimidating, even as the sun began to sink. The smell of sage was stronger, and I heard gentle murmurs, low and smooth. I began to relax as we continued through. There was no shouting, no tension, only an even flow.

Perhaps this won't be so bad.

I placed a hand on the trunk of a tree as I continued forward. My other hand held on to my skirts, careful not to trip over anything on the ground.

We emerged again, this time into a little grove I didn't know existed. Fireflies lit up the grove like candles in the night, lighting up the darkness and leading the way. Sage filled the air, but also something else. Incense, I realized. Mother sometimes burned incense throughout our home. She said it was to ward evil spirits from entering. Father always teased her, but she was serious about the protection. It seemed to work, nonetheless.

Other women, dressed in long dresses and pantaloons, in clinging material, walked barefoot. Some were talking, others were alone, working on their magic. Tendrils of bold colors pierced the dimness, and magic lit up this area of the forest. There was a large fire pit in the center of the circle, the flames licking the night sky as embers crackled and popped. The smell of something salty pierced my nose, smothering the strong scent of sage. Something was being roasted.

At that moment, my stomach rumbled, and I realized just how hungry I was. Lizzie chuckled, coming up behind me. "Isn't it grand?" she asked in a low murmur.

I could do nothing but nod. The truth was it was grand. These women were free to do as they wished, to be who they wanted. They didn't seem concerned in the slightest about Patrol stumbling upon their activities. No one even looked up as Lizzie and I emerged from the forest.

"This is my coven," Thaya said, coming up behind me. "And you, Hannah, are a Legacy."

"A Legacy?" I asked. "I have no relation to the king of Cardonia—"

"Not that," she snapped. "What do I care of trivial hierarchies created by man? You are a Legacy to this coven. Our great ancestor Eve began it before she was found and burned alive at the stake. Since then, the women in our family have been part of it for centuries. And now, you are here. You can see it for yourself."

"How has no one discovered this?" I asked before I could stop myself. Fireflies danced around me. One tousled itself in my hair. I jumped, not fond of insects, even ones with no intention of harming me.

"Oh, we are well-known throughout Ankura," Thaya said as she weaved her fingers through my hair to remove the firefly. "We sell our trinkets in the square every night, protection charms, love potions. They know of us. But they fear us. There is an unspoken rule: as long as we don't use our magick outside of the forest, we are free to do as we please."

"Brendan Pickard is okay with that arrangement?" I asked in surprise, shifting my eyes to Lizzie. She and the lieutenant of Ankura's chapter of Patrol had been engaged for a brief moment before Brendan broke the engagement without any explanation as to why. A shame, too, because Brendan was a good man and Lizzie had never been happier.

"Lieutenant Pickard knows nothing of it," Thaya said. "And we answer to no one."

I frowned. "I thought you said—"

"The agreement stands because it benefits us now," Thaya said. "But we will not be cast in the shadows any longer. Witches must be free to be who they are without the worry of death hanging above our heads. And we will be." She locked eyes with me. "Enough talk of this, dear niece. I'm glad you have come. Let me introduce you to everyone, and then you can return home."

"I thought, perhaps, I could train—" I started.

"And you will," Thaya insisted, placing a hand on my shoulder. "But not now." Her smile contained a hint of command. "You aren't ready yet."

CHAPTER FIVE

Hannah

On my return, as I stepped through the foyer doors of the manor house, I didn't expect to see the foreboding presence of Adrian Blood. I stumbled, knocking the side table, the vase he'd once studied with intensity when he'd first paid me a visit wobbling dangerously. I stayed it with a trembling hand. Why was he here? It was past proper visiting hours and he knew it.

Lizzie too was in the foyer, no doubt waiting for me to arrive. I looked at her, wondering what she felt about his presence, as her hazel eyes searched Adrian's face. Her lips curved down, and she moved slightly to position herself in front of me, likely because she believed she could protect me from him.

If only she knew.

Adrian's eyes followed Lizzie's movements. He didn't seem perturbed, but I knew Adrian; he took in much more than he let on.

"Ms. Walker," Adrian said, turning to give my sister his attention. He bowed his head slightly. "You look lovely this evening."

"Even though I let you in because that is a common courtesy, I must tell you our father has retired for the evening," Lizzie said. Her voice was firm; she left no room to be toyed with. If anything, she sounded more like Brendan Pickard of Patrol, though I wouldn't dare tell her such a thing. "I doubt you would wish Harold to wake him unless it is an utmost emergency?" She arched a brow in a silent challenge.

"It *is* an emergency," Adrian said, "though it is not your father I must speak to." He turned and stared pointedly at me. "Ms. Walker—"

"No." Lizzie's voice filled the foyer in defiance.

I turned to stare at her, but she was glaring at Adrian. Her lips were pursed into a thin line, hands framing her waist, shoulders rigid and unflinching. This was her power stance, one she employed whenever she could feel an argument coming on. She was not easily pushed around. The fact she could look Adrian Blood directly in the eye and glare at him was no small feat. Even I had to admit she was fearless in certain circumstances, to the point of stupidity.

"I apologize," Adrian said, taking a casual step forward. "I wasn't asking you. I will only accept responses from her." He tilted his head in my direction.

Lizzie looked as though she wanted to argue. I saw her lift her index finger, then set it down, then lift it again…like some kind of nervous tic.

No, not a tic. Her magick. She was readying her magick in case she felt she must use it.

I couldn't let that happen, though whether it was to protect Lizzie or to protect Adrian, I didn't know. Perhaps it was a bit of both.

"Lizzie, it will only be for a moment," I said quickly. Though I spoke to my sister, I couldn't remove my gaze from Adrian's ice-blue eyes. It was as though he had me under some sort of spell. "I will see what he wants and then he will leave. That's all."

The corners of Adrian's lips tilted up, almost as though to say, "Will I?"

Lizzie pursed her lips, looking between the two of us. I could tell she didn't want to let me see Adrian alone. Whether that was because she didn't trust him with me, or because she didn't trust me with him, I couldn't say.

In truth, I didn't care. My curiosity was piqued. I wanted to know what brought Adrian here after all these months.

I tried not to think about the way he stared at me, especially since I was certain I was staring at him the same way as well. I'd seen Adrian on multiple occasions. I should be used to the striking beauty he possessed, wrapped up in masculine brutality both intimidating and alluring. He was taller than I was, with sweeping broad shoulders and a compact frame. He always dressed in the finest of clothing; the clothes hugged him like a second skin, all tailored to his measurements. Even the black boots on his feet were polished so well I was certain I would be able to see my reflection.

His short, fair hair was pushed from his face, only revealing the sharp edges of his cheeks, his jaw. There was something about his stare, his focus. It made me feel as though I was the only person in this room with him, even though Lizzie was there.

"Shall I receive you in the library?" I asked. It was the only place I could think of where there was a good chance I wouldn't be overwhelmed by his presence. There was enough space to keep a proper distance between us.

"You may receive me wherever you like," he said lazily.

His low, sultry voice crawled over my skin, and I remembered his fingers once doing the same thing. I shivered, remembering how soft they were, and yet, there was power in them. I knew, if he truly wanted to, he could turn my bones to ash.

"Hannah, I don't think—" Lizzie said.

"Mr. Blood is Father's client," I said firmly, turning to give my sister a stern look. "I don't tell you to dismiss any of your blacksmith clients when they come to the manor."

"None have come to my home," Lizzie said. "There are lines."

"All lines are meant to be crossed, Ms. Walker," Adrian said, sauntering toward me, hands behind his back. "I'm certain you know this personally."

Lizzie paled under Adrian's knowing look but she didn't flinch. "I shall remain here in case you need anything, Hannah," she said. Though she spoke to me, her eyes were on my guest.

"I appreciate it, but that won't be necessary." I continued to lead Adrian to the library, my heart throbbing with a mix of apprehension and forbidden delight.

I wondered if he could hear it with his fine auditory sense and wrinkled my nose.

Of course, he can.

I tried not to think about what else he might pick up on as I led him down the hallway. I wished I was able to read his thoughts the way Lizzie could. Perhaps that was why she was so intent on staying with me, because she had read his thoughts and perceived him as a threat. But if that were the case, she'd never have let me go with him no matter how much I insisted.

I should perhaps warn Adrian about her ability. He couldn't risk exposure. My little voice spoke smugly. *After everything, you still long to protect him?*

I ignored it. When I reached the door, I opened it and stepped through, knowing he'd follow me no matter where I led him.

The door clicked shut, and only then did I turn, watching as Adrian locked us inside. My eyes narrowed, and my heartbeat quickened. While I understood the necessity for closing the door, I didn't know why he would lock it.

"Is there a problem?" he asked smoothly. I gathered my skirts in my hands and took a seat on the edge of my father's leather couch.

"Why would there be?" I asked, my voice cracking. I cleared my throat. "Mr. Blood—"

"Save the trivialities," he snapped. "I don't wish to hear you call me by such formalities, not when I know you so…intimately."

"What do you want?" I demanded. I didn't like the effect his voice had on my body. My fingers curled around the leather seat as I attempted to ignore the heat that seared through my body.

"What were you going to say just now?" Adrian positioned himself in front of me, standing just before the wooden coffee table that still had books on its surface from the last time I came here. "Before I interrupted you."

"Oh," I said after a moment. "I just wanted to warn you…Lizzie's powers are much stronger than my own. She can read thoughts, and I wanted to warn you to be careful what you projected around her. As I'm sure you're aware, she doesn't trust you, and now she's been working more and more with Aunt Thaya, I'm certain her power is only going to get stronger."

Adrian was silent for a moment. "Your sister is learning magick from your aunt?" he asked, his voice crisp.

"Yes," I said slowly. "Why, is that a problem?"

"Do you know your aunt and her coven feast on magick from outsiders?" he asked.

I blinked once, then twice. "I'm sorry?" I asked. I couldn't have heard him correctly.

"Your aunt," he repeated, "feasts on others' magick to make herself grow more powerful. Surely you know this. There is a reason she lives in the forest. She wishes to do magick, to grow stronger, so one day she can exact her revenge."

My mind tried to keep up with everything Adrian was telling me. Was he telling me my aunt was…bad? I knew I didn't trust her, not yet. But when she went over information with me, when she discussed my magick and brought up my own, she always seemed excited her nieces were finally stepping into themselves. It made me let my guard down around her, just slightly, because she seemed happy for us.

Could that be because she wanted to use our magick for some nefarious purpose like Adrian seemed to be suggesting?

I didn't want to discuss this with him. It wasn't any of his business what I did or didn't do with my magick or my aunt, who was still family. It was my magick, my family blood after all, and I could do what I wanted with them both.

"Revenge for what?" I asked.

"She still holds humans responsible for the near-extinction of her kind," Adrian said. "The fact she and her coven of witches are relegated to the Forest of Legend to do their magick, as if they are nothing more than animals, doesn't sit right with her. And let's not forget if any of them are caught, the law supports their arrest and execution."

"And you think she wants revenge for all of that?" I asked, picking at the leather seat.

"I *know* she does." His eyes lingered on my face, and in the candlelight, I noticed something flicker across them; something protective, almost territorial.

I stood up, taking the books I left scattered on the coffee table with me. I needed to put them away, distract myself.

"Why do you run from me?" Adrian asked as I ducked behind a row of books.

"Why do you look at me so?" I asked in return. My voice sounded undecided and I wished I could be stronger.

"And how do I look at you?"

Suddenly, he was behind me. I didn't know how I knew it, but I did. He wasn't even touching me and the back of my neck prickled with anticipation. I tried to moisten my throat, but my mouth was dry.

"Well?" His fingers found my wrist and he gave me a gentle tug until I turned toward him. He took the books from my hands and set them on the shelf behind him. His eyes burned into mine with a need to hear my answer. "Tell me. How do I look at you?"

"Like you possess every inch of me," I said. The words came out before I could stop them. I wanted to swallow them back down, but it was too late.

Adrian leaned forward, his gaze dipping to my mouth. Suddenly, I was certain he was going to kiss me again. He was going to claim my lips and make my body set itself on fire. He was going to consume me, and I would be little more than flaming cinders at his feet.

I should leave. I should run away. But I was rooted in place. The truth was, I wanted him to kiss me. I wanted him to claim me.

But he didn't press his lips to mine. Instead, he leaned in close, close enough to touch.

"Would you like me to possess every inch of you, Hannah?" he murmured. My breathing deepened and I tried to get control of my rapidly beating heart.

"What do you want?" My voice came out as a pathetic whisper, and I couldn't stop it from cracking.

"What if I said I came here just to see you?" he asked, tilting his head to the side. However, he still stayed too close for my liking.

"I would call you a liar," I said.

He arched an insolent brow. "Because your magick told you so?" he asked.

"I don't need my magick to tell me that," I replied. "You're here for a reason, and it has nothing to do with me."

"That's where you're wrong, little fool," Adrian said. He brought his hand up and pressed his palm against the column of my throat. Long fingers weaved around my neck. He wasn't threatening me; this was a gentle caress. "It has everything to do with you." A beat. "I need your help."

I forgot for a moment I was trapped in Adrian's grasp. "Are you all right?" I asked without thinking.

Adrian stilled, eyes widening. "Be careful, darling," he said in a low voice. "You almost sound as though you care."

I looked away. I hated I cared at that moment. I hated I couldn't even deny it.

"Some of the Sirens are missing," he said after another moment of lingering silence. He dropped his hand from my throat and took a step back. I could breathe again. "I believe someone intercepted them before they could be delivered to me. I need your help to figure out what happened to them."

"The Sirens you're going to use at your brothel?" I asked, my mind working again now he wasn't touching me, was not quite so near. "They've disappeared?"

He nodded once.

"I can't help you, Adrian," I said. "I won't. I don't want you to participate in such evil. And if the Sirens found a way to get out of their current predicament, I would help them."

"You don't understand—"

"My answer is no," I said firmly, surprised by my confident tone. "Was there anything else?"

Adrian's mouth thinned. His eyes narrowed. Something flashed across his eyes, something looking almost like pain. But it was gone before I could confirm. Without another word, he turned and left.

CHAPTER SIX

Adrian

Heat trailed up my body, and my muscles tensed in response to Hannah's dismissal. My blood surged beneath my skin, boiling with rage,

How dare she, that little hussy.

I clenched my teeth, already feeling my incisors push out, wanting nothing more than to tear into something, to rip flesh from body, to drown myself in hot, sticky-sweet blood and listen as the pulse it belonged to slowed until it stopped completely.

I couldn't react in front of her. I hated she was the catalyst for such emotions, or that I felt such emotions in the first place. I was used to remaining uncaring about most of my encounters unless someone attacked me or offended me. Hannah Walker was the only thing that ever made me feel more than I had before, and I hated her for it.

I had no choice but to leave her home. If Reginald Walker awoke, he would demand to know what was going on. He knew about the girls, about what I did, but I couldn't risk him knowing some of the girls were gone. What if he was behind it? I needed to figure this out on my own.

I had hoped Hannah would assist. She was a bleeding heart for those girls. I still remembered the lecture she gave me in her bedroom the night she saved my life from Pepper. I growled, just thinking about that caustic bitch, the only person I'd trusted before I knew she'd betrayed me to the Pascals. She wanted to kill me so she could take my place. Her naivety led her to believe such a thing was possible. And it almost was…if Hannah hadn't put her own life in danger to save mine.

Foolish, incredible little mortal.

Frustration burned through my body as I left the Walker Mansion. I hadn't seen her in months, and yet, the mere instant I was with her in person, suddenly I was no longer an intimidating Blood Mage, but someone else.

I needed her help. I needed her assistance with this…and she refused. I hadn't expected that. Perhaps I should be thanking her. If I was this caught up in the swell of emotions after one short visit, what would happen if we worked together once more?

I made my way back to the forest. Because Hannah refused to offer her assistance didn't mean I was free from needing it.

I didn't trust the witches. I didn't trust the other Blood Mages, whether I knew them personally because they frequented my brothel or not. I didn't even trust the Pascals with the information I discovered, certain they would uncover the truth of what I was doing if they were to find out.

Our agreement was I collected the girls, got them to the brothel, and started them working. Which I did. But what nobody knew was then I began to siphon them out, freeing one or two girls at a time. Not even Hannah.

It was a slow process, and I never released more than two girls a month, sometimes even longer. I couldn't risk anyone finding out what I was doing, especially after Pepper had. And what she'd done to the humans working with me, assisting the Sirens in getting free.

Both wound up dead, so I was on my own. For now.

My only other option for uncovering information was from the Lost. They too lived in the forest, but there was a cave just off to the side, near the cliffs that overlooked the eastern part of the ocean. There, they could frolic and hunt wildlife with minimal risk of being spotted, whether by a witch, a human, or a Blood Mage.

Charles Rochester was their unofficial leader, and despite being turned into a Blood Mage, there was something remarkably human about him. He was not quite feral, not animalistic, though, perhaps, he had better control of it than most in his position did. However, there was a chance he might be willing to help me, and while I wasn't one to ask for assistance, I didn't have a choice in the matter.

It took me a quarter of an hour to get to where I wanted to go. Once I emerged from the thicket of trees, I noticed three Lost men, all at the edge of the Devil's Mouth, the cave the Lost inhabited. They looked tense, as though they had been expecting my presence. They wouldn't act without orders from their leader, however. Of that, I was certain.

And if they did, I was able to handle three of them. Though they were more feral than Blood Mages, I had been alive a lot longer than most, which meant my powers had heightened with age.

Part of me hoped they would do something as foolish as an attack. I needed any excuse to rip into something after being turned down by Hannah.

None of the Lost spoke to me. I knew it wasn't because they were incapable. They were. Rochester himself could pass as the human he used to be, should he want to. Despite the fact he was a pyrate, Rochester was born into a wealthy family and was highly educated. No one knew why he turned pyrate, however, and I didn't care enough to ask.

"I need to speak to your leader," I called to them, maintaining my distance. They would perceive anything as a threat and I didn't want to stroke their ire, even if I was feeling more aggressive than usual.

The Lost just stared at me. They didn't even blink. I waited, not letting them intimidate me.

After a long moment, a silhouette appeared at the mouth of the cave until Charles Rochester himself stepped out. His blue gaze contemplated me, studying me, no doubt wondering why I was here.

I waited. Let him think what he wanted. The night was young, though if we continued to waste any more time, I would be forced to speed this along, and I didn't like to rush things.

Finally, Charles tilted his chin up. I was taller and broader than he was, but still, he commanded respect. "What are you doing here?" he asked in his low, gravelly voice.

"We have a problem," I said. I glanced over at the others before looking back at him. "Can we speak privately?"

"I'm not sure I can trust myself alone with Adrian Blood," Charles said, amusement dancing in his gaze. "It would be too tempting to kill him and deliver his head to the Pascals. They want you dead, don't they?"

"Perhaps," I said nonchalantly, "but they need me, and you know why."

Charles glanced over to his men and gave them a silent nod. Immediately, the men retreated into the mouth of the cave as Charles walked toward me.

"I wonder what it would be worth to them if I delivered them your head myself," he murmured.

"I'm worth more alive, at least for the time being," I said. "And if you think you can win the Pascals' favor simply by killing me, I suggest you get the notion out of your head. You will always be a Lost Mage. Always. You were turned. Your men were turned. Just because you kill me, that won't change. Do not be naive."

"I know what I am," Charles said through gritted teeth. "You need to remember who *you* are."

"And what's that?"

"A tool," he said with a sneer. "A pawn. A bitch. You do everything your master bids you to do. Should he kick your side, you'll take the brunt of the pain and thank him for it. You regard me as someone less than you. I started as human, to be sure, but whether I was a pyrate or a Blood Mage, I've never let anyone take advantage of me the way you've done."

I growled, taking a menacing step forward. Charles rolled his shoulders back but otherwise didn't move. He tilted his chin up and maintained eye contact. There was a glimmer of trepidation in his eyes. But I wouldn't say he was afraid of me.

The fool should be.

"What are you doing here?" he asked.

"Have your men been intercepting my Sirens?" I asked. The time for niceties had passed. I didn't wish to waste more time here than I already had.

"Excuse me?" This time, the words weren't offended; he seemed truly perplexed.

"I'm missing a handful of Sirens," I said. "Two, to be precise. And we've had trouble before where your Lost would intercept my deliveries and feast on them as though they were little more than animals."

"Isn't that how you treat them?" Charles asked, arching a brow.

"I will not stand here and have you question what I do and how I do it," I snapped. "I need to know if they're doing it again."

"I told them to stop," Charles said. "They've stopped. We feast only on the animals that make up this forest. If anyone defied my orders, I would know."

I wasn't sure he would. I didn't understand how he managed to keep the Lost in line when they could barely control themselves.

"Would you?" I glanced down and began to pace up and down the length of the Devil's Mouth, careful not to cross over and give Charles the impression I was on the attack. Despite the tension between us, we were having a civilized conversation, and I didn't want to ruin that. "Tonight, I was informed two girls are missing. I had no delivery at all for the month."

Charles didn't look perturbed. "And why does that stun you so?" he asked. "Perhaps Underedge has stopped sending you Sirens completely."

"They would not," I said.

"And why's that?"

"The king entered into this deal with the Pascals, not Ankura," I informed him. I didn't know if it was a good idea to divulge such sensitive information to Charles but I didn't feel as though I had a choice. "I doubt the king would renege on that, knowing there would be dire consequences."

"And what sort of consequences would they be?" Charles asked curiously.

"War, for one," I said. "Surely you've heard the rumors, even if you are here living in the Devil's Mouth. I know you frequent the town. I know in particular, you visit the oldest Beckett girl. She might not know you're there, but I do."

Charles locked his jaw so tightly that it popped. I almost smiled. Everyone had a weakness, even animalistic Lost Mages. What Charles's fascination with Jessa Beckett was, I didn't know. But I knew knowing would work to my benefit in some way.

"Tell me," I said breezily, dropping my gaze to the back of my hand. I fiddled with the sleeve of my tunic. "What is she to you? A lover, perhaps? A victim? Or both?"

Charles remained silent, but his nostrils flared. I knew that would be the only warning I received from him, a warning I should probably listen to.

"She is something to you, though," I continued, dropping my arms back to my sides. "I'm sure no one else knows you're there. I doubt even she does, or else she might close that balcony window. If she knew you lingered just outside her room—a monster wrapped up in the trappings of a human—she might use the magick she possesses to kill you. Unless one of her sisters does it first."

"Let's not discuss little witchlings and the feelings they stir in Blood Mages," Charles said slowly. "You might have discovered something about me, but everyone knows about your weakness in Hannah Walker. You can deny it all you want, Blood. But *she* is something to *you*, even if you can't name it. Which just begs the question—why are you here, asking for my help, when you could be asking her?" He raised his brow, an idea dawning on him. "Unless you already asked, and she rejected you."

My fangs wanted to slide out of my mouth but I held them back with a soft snarl.

Charles noticed my frustration. His eyes widened; lips curled into a smirk. "So," he said. "That's it, then. You went to her, she rejected you…and you're angry about it." Charles's lips twisted up. "She's under your skin, mate."

"Desist in speaking of her, and I will do the same about Jessa Beckett," I said tautly.

Charles's smirk deepened but he nodded once. "What do you want, Blood Mage? I already told you my men haven't intercepted any deliveries. Take my word or don't, but the answer is still the same."

"The delivery boy said he never received the Sirens," I said. "I believe someone stole them."

"Who'd want to do such a thing?" Charles asked.

"That's what I must find out."

Charles nodded. "And you want *my* help to do it."

I kept silent. *I'm not going to beg him for assistance.*

"All right," he said after a moment. "I'll help. But I want something in return."

I sneered. Of course he did. "And what is that?"

"A favor," Charles said. "To be used at my discretion." He stuck out his hand. "Do we have a deal?"

I stared at his hand before slowly placing mine in his. I had no choice in the matter, not if I wanted to discover the truth of what was happening with the Sirens.

CHAPTER SEVEN

Hannah

The next morning, I woke from a slumber I didn't get to fully enjoy. My mind had been filled with Adrian, his perfect face, the way he looked at me with icy blue eyes. He was pleading with me in my dream, pleading for my assistance, and I rejected him.

My chest squeezed tightly, paralyzing me with pain that was riddled with emotions I couldn't shake off. I pressed my palm flat on the center of my chest, hoping that would help ease the ache, but it did nothing. I was forced to remain in my bed until it passed.

Lizzie was probably already returning to Aunt Thaya and the coven. I was glad when she made no move to get me to go with her. I had yet to decide if I wanted to participate in those rituals.

I stretched, sitting up against my headboard. Guilt swam through me. Thaya was my mother's sister. Never had Mother spoken ill of her, and yet…there was something about her I didn't quite trust. Perhaps it was Marcella's words of needing to learn and accept my magick without outside help. Perhaps it was Adrian's lingering warning about Thaya and her witches itself. Whatever it was had caused me to hesitate around my forest-dwelling aunt. I didn't like the way it made me feel.

I glanced over at the door, hoping I might be able to detect if someone was coming to rouse me from my slumber. I knew Father was especially distracted with news of impending war and collecting protection fees on businesses. As much as I adored my father, I didn't think it fair to take advantage of businesses in such troubling times.

I looked down at my fingers, wishing I knew exactly what to do to make my magick work. When I'd been saving Adrian, the thought of losing him had caused the magick in me to flow naturally. Part of me didn't understand why, and part of me did. I'd already accepted I cared for Adrian and my emotions played a part in generating my magick somehow. Even though months had passed between us, that hadn't diminished what I felt for him. I'd known it the second I'd seen him again when we'd spoken in the library last night. My heart raced just thinking about it, warming my cheeks.

I wanted to see him again…and I didn't.

I threw the covers off my body, stepped onto the floor, and the harsh cold from the winter floors rippled through my body. I yelped. I detested the cold, especially when I was still half-asleep. The only good to come out of it was the fact I was distracted from thoughts of Adrian.

Until I moved to my wardrobe and noticed the clothing he had once given me folded and tucked away in the corner, where not even Roseanna could see them. My gaze lingered. He'd given me those during an especially rainy night when my dress was completely soaked through. I'd changed in the same room as him after he'd assisted in unlacing my corset. Even now, I could still feel his fingers on my back, and a shudder slid down my spine the way one of his fingers might have.

"He's not a good man," I said out loud, trying to shake my thoughts from my unexpected wistfulness.

And yet, I couldn't help but think back to yesterday, to what brought him to me in the first place. His missing shipment of girls. That itself was not something I cared about. I meant what I said. I wanted them to go missing, to be free of a life they couldn't possibly want.

But then I thought of poor dead Claire, she who had been a great judge of character. I thought of the dead girl Jonathan Nyx was blamed for. They, too, had been working for Adrian, willingly helping him free the girls. Both had met with unfortunate ends. Both killings remained unsolved, though most still believed it was Nyx.

Adrian seemed forced to play this game he was mixed up in, which meant he was working for someone powerful. Besides my father and my uncle, Adrian was the most powerful man I knew. Who could intimidate a Blood Mage?

The only person Adrian seemed concerned about was Diego Pascal. A fleeting memory lifted my hand to caress my face. He'd once threatened me, drawing blood with a blade pressed to my cheek.

Perhaps Adrian's fear stemmed from the fact Diego Pascal possessed power over Adrian. Could Adrian be working for *him*?

I wrinkled my nose at the thought. I couldn't see how Adrian would allow himself to fall into such an arrangement. I couldn't picture him taking orders from anyone.

Today I preferred peace as I readied myself for the day—or what was left of it. I removed my clothing and changed into a dress I pulled from my closet, lacing up the corset behind me as best as I could. A plan started to form in my brain. I needed to leave the house without running into anyone. Hopefully, Lizzie would be at her blacksmith shop, but Father might be around. I hoped though he was still distracted by the prospective war coming to our shores shortly.

I felt a little guilty, thinking I should be more concerned about it too, but I didn't have a true sense of how serious it was. People seemed to be sheltering me from it. Lizzie hadn't told me anything more about what she knew since the day she'd caught me sneaking inside from visiting Marcella. I was grateful she hadn't spotted Sage with me, as I was sure she would have a lot more questions.

I shook my head and took a seat at my bureau. I couldn't do anything about war. That wasn't something within my control.

But visiting Brendan Pickard at Fort Crimson was. Perhaps he would know if there were new girls populating Ankura who smelled distinctly of salt, brine, and fish.

***

Getting out of the house later that evening was easier than I thought. No one was around to notice me, not even Sage, who always seemed to be around at the most inopportune time, being nosy and fishing for any information he could.

The day was not warm, the air crisp with a hint of salt on it. The sun was already descending. It wouldn't be dark though for a little while, which meant Adrian was still on his ship. I cast my eyes wistfully to the ocean even though I knew his ship was on the other, more isolated side of the island.

My heart skipped a beat at the thought of him. I curled my fingers into fists, digging my nails into the fleshy part of my palm.

Stop thinking about him.

I shook my head and began to make my way down the hill and into town. It was bustling with people—mothers taking their daughters shopping for dresses for their debuts, fathers and sons fishing at the docks or taking their dinner from work. I moved amongst them, blending in. I felt like one of them, as if I wasn't a Walker or someone with a dark, deadly secret of uncontrolled magick coursing through me.

By the time I made it to Fort Crimson, my fingernails had pierced crescents into my palms from gripping so tight. I didn't want to have my magick triggered if someone bumped into me accidentally.

I opened the heavy door and stepped into the small Patrol office within the fort. It still smelled of stale alcohol, the scent overwhelming to the point where I lifted one hand and covered my nose. Lanterns lit the dark room. I took a couple of steps forward, trying to peer into the darkness.

"Hello?" a familiar voice called. "Anyone there?"

My shoulders sagged with relief. I didn't want to admit the darkness had frightened me so Brendan Pickard's voice was a welcome sound.

"Brendan? It's me. Hannah Walker."

It took another moment before my eyes adjusted to the room, but once they did, I felt comfortable moving around with ease. I stepped forward until I found his desk. It was still scattered with parchment and spilt ink. I didn't see any empty bottles of alcohol Henry Davenport, Brendan's Lead within Patrol, might have finished off. I wanted to take that as a good sign, but Henry had stopped drinking before and it never quite stuck.

"Hannah," Brendan said, standing up as I approached. "I'm surprised you're here."

"Why?" I asked, genuinely curious. The two of us had a history. Well, he and Lizzie did. I knew him through Lizzie and had liked him very much. He seemed to be the only man on Ankura to truly understand her. Until she'd called off their engagement rather abruptly.

"Considering I accused you of murdering your best friend, I doubted you'd want anything to do with me," he pointed out in his deep, melodic voice.

I nodded, placing my hands loosely behind my back. He wasn't wrong. Brendan had dared to say Richard—Claire's betrothed—and I were engaged in a secret affair, and one of us killed Claire to rid ourselves of her while he was in my home. After everything we'd been through together, despite how well he knew me, the fact he could think I could do something as vile as that was insulting and had hurt me more than I was willing to say.

"Tell me, how's the real affair you're engaged in going?" This time, his voice was nothing short of sarcastic, the look in his blue eyes flat.

I knew he was referring to Adrian Blood.

"I haven't seen the two of you together in the past couple of months," he continued. There was a small, arrogant bite to his tone.

He's been around Henry far too much.

He carried on. "Is everything still right in paradise?"

"Quite frankly, Brendan, it's none of your concern," I said haughtily, trying to hide my annoyance. "And you have yet to apologize for your baseless accusations."

"Is that why you're here, then?" he challenged. "You want an apology?"

"Actually, no." I reached his desk and placed my hands on the parchment that rested on its surface. They crunched under my weight. "I'm here because I wanted to ask you whether or not you've heard of girls going missing."

"Girls?" He arched a brow. "Unfortunately, girls go missing all the time. Pyrates snatch away the wealthy ones for a ransom or two. The impoverished lose girls all the time. It happens more—"

"I mean, those who work at the brothel," I said.

Brendan pressed his lips together and gave me a long look, no doubt studying my face to try to see more of what I knew.

"The brothel," he said finally, his tone flat. "Why concern yourself with them? Is this a jealousy thing? If Mr. Blood is receiving his pleasure from them and not you, that doesn't mean they're missing."

I curled my fingers in the parchment, bending and tearing the material. I didn't realize I'd have such a strong reaction to what Brendan was saying until he said it, but I didn't like the thought of Adrian with those girls.

"Forget it," I said. My magick was too close to the surface. I couldn't risk it. I released the parchment and took a step back from the desk, afraid if I didn't put space between us, something bad might happen.

I headed toward the door. *I knew this was a bad idea. I shouldn't have wasted my time.*

"Hannah."

I froze under Brendan's commanding tone and turned slowly to look at him.

"Don't get yourself mixed up with the likes of Adrian Blood," he said, his tone serious. "Do you love him?"

I was unsure how to answer. Brendan looked away, something flashing in his eyes. It would seem my silence was answer enough.

"Love makes us do things we can't comprehend," he said. "I shall answer your question, but only because I think it's a sufficient deterrent against him." He hesitated. "Remember the woman who drowned, the one we pulled out of the ocean and it was reported Nyx was responsible for?"

I nodded. "I remember. Even though I don't believe it was Nyx."

Brendan glared but didn't contradict me. "There was a witness who mentioned she saw the girl with three other women, all getting into the ocean," he said. "To her, it looked like they were trying to escape something, but she didn't say what. Henry thought she was drunk, but I've seen drunk before, and I know she believed she was telling the truth."

"So," I said, wrinkling my nose. "The girl who died. She...she was getting girls into the water?"

"The witness said the instant they touched the water, they grew tails and swam away, leaving the woman who later died by herself," he said. "Of course, we couldn't verify her claim. It sounded ridiculous, even to us. But, Hannah, these girls were described wearing what the girls at the brothel wear. I can't prove it, but I'm almost certain Adrian Blood is responsible for that girl's death. The one who didn't transform into a mermaid. Perhaps he discovered she was trying to free them, helping them escape from the business."

"I...I appreciate you telling me this," I told him honestly.

"I know things didn't end well between me and your sister," he said, "but I still think of you like family, Hannah. I still care. About both of you. Take caution around Adrian Blood. He is not a good man."

No, Adrian was not a good man. He was not a man at all. But I still had to tell him what Brendan told me. I gave him a quick curtsey and left, hoping the sun had set and I would not need to wait long to see Adrian.

CHAPTER EIGHT

Hannah

I shouldn't be here. I knew this. Every instinct I possessed screamed at me, begging me to return home where it was safe.

But I knew I'd do no such thing.

This was Adrian, and I'd do everything I could to help him, even if it meant putting myself in danger. I couldn't rely on any help—save for a Blood Mage who probably hated me at this point after my cold rejection.

I reached the entrance of the brothel and took a deep breath. *It's not like you've never been here before*, I silently reminded myself. *This is just one stop on your father's route. And since you're poised to take over his business, you should be comfortable being here.*

The words came easy, but it was difficult to believe in them. I arched my back, tilted my chin up, and curled my fingers around the doorknob to push it open. The brothel itself looked the same as it always had. The foyer was empty, save for a few girls who worked here positioning themselves seductively on the staircase. The second they recognised me, they relaxed, knowing I wasn't a potential client.

To my left, there was a lobby with a bar and seats for clients to have a drink and socialize before they received the services they came for. I knew it wasn't only humans who frequented this place; it was a mix of humans and Blood Mages who came to get intimate with a girl but also to feed from them.

My stomach turned just thinking about it.

I hated Adrian in that moment. How I could care so much about someone who did such wretched things?

Perhaps he doesn't have *a choice,* a voice in my head pointed out.

Hmm, I thought. There was always a choice. What someone did with that choice was what mattered. And Adrian—Adrian had made his choice.

I turned to the lobby. I doubted Adrian would be present, but I never knew what to expect from him. The floor was crowded with people as nighttime was the busiest time for the brothel. I hoped no one recognized me.

I couldn't have my father finding out I was here in the first place. Or Lizzie, or Thaya, for that matter.

"What are you doing here anyway?" I muttered to myself, shaking my head at the ridiculousness of my choices. "Why do you think you can help him?"

Because he asked me to, my inner voice reminded me.

I curled my hair behind my ear, having left it down. It was a last-minute decision as I hoped it might mask my features and hide me.

My eyes searched through the crowd of people, but I couldn't see Adrian. I took the only vacant seat at the bar. The bartender came and asked for my drink order but I waved him away politely. I didn't want to be noticed or interact with anyone. If I didn't see Adrian in the next few minutes, I'd leave, satisfied I'd at least made the effort to come.

I glanced up and looked up the stairs. The girls who'd been there were gone, vanishing surprisingly quickly. Perhaps they'd disappeared to their rooms when they didn't get a customer or received a customer and I was too deep in my thoughts to realize it.

A few seconds later, a couple of people descended the staircase. One was a beautiful woman with bright, blonde hair and deep blue eyes. She was petite but had a commanding presence, one I thought wistfully I could never hope to duplicate. Behind her was Adrian himself, too close to the blonde goddess for my personal preference.

His chest was pressed into her back, his head dipped so he could whisper in her ear. I didn't like the way she angled her head away from him so it seemed he could caress her throat with his lips should he want to. I didn't like the way his eyes seemed focused on only her.

I took a deep breath. She was beautiful. Why shouldn't he enjoy her? I didn't own the man.

But the thought of him doing anything intimate, even something as innocent as this public display of affection, caused my skin to turn to fire. Before I knew it, magick shot out of me and the glass pints behind the bar burst into pieces.

Everyone froze. My breath left me.

Adrian's gaze immediately shot to mine. How he found me so quickly in the crowd, I didn't know. The entire lobby went still.

I tried to hold his heated stare as my body trembled in both apprehension and need.

"Out," Adrian commanded as he pulled away from the girl and walked down the stairs. "Everyone out. Now."

Somehow, I knew I wasn't included in his instruction. I remained frozen in my seat, unable to look away. I had heard the rumor Blood Mages possessed some sort of secret magick, the kind that captivated and paralyzed, the kind that persuaded and pleased. One a person wouldn't even realize was being used on them.

I wondered if Adrian was using that magick now.

He didn't move until everyone had left and as far as I could tell, we were completely alone. Only then did he stride toward me, his presence overwhelming. I felt the pull toward him, the desire to be swept up in his arms. I placed my hands on the edge of the bar and gripped down hard, hoping it would keep me seated.

"What are you doing here?" he asked when he was behind the bar, in front of me.

"I…I have information for you," I said.

"Would this information be why you shattered my glasses?" He glanced at the mess, still on the surface of the bar, and behind it.

"Tell me, it wouldn't have to do with the fact you saw me with a beautiful woman on my arm, would it?" A small smirk danced on his lips and for a moment, I forgot who he was and had the sudden urge to slap it off his chiseled face.

"Of course not," I insisted, but the words sounded hollow, even to my ears. "I don't care what you do with your time nor who you do it with."

"I may not possess your natural talent at knowing when someone is lying, but you, my darling, are," he said. Confidence laced his tone, enraging me further. "You saw me with Hessie and it irked you so much, you lost control of your magick and broke my glasses." He reached out and traced the column of my throat with his fingers, the same place he'd kissed me in my room, way back then. I shivered. "You have nothing to fear, you know. She means nothing to me. Not the way you do."

"Yes, clearly," I said without thinking. I pulled away from him and forced myself to stand up.

Adrian's smirk only deepened. "You are jealous," he said. "Your nerves are frazzled. You can't even sit still at the thought of me with someone else. This is an interesting development."

"And why is that?" I asked sharply. I paced the small length of space behind my seat, needing to empty all this sudden excess energy I had.

"Because I didn't think you cared," he said.

"I don't," I snapped. It sounded pathetic, even to me. "You know, I came here for a reason, but if all you want to do is play these ridiculous games, I can leave."

I turned and headed for the exit, but I'd only taken two steps before Adrian was in front of me, entirely too close. He took a step forward and I took a step back. I couldn't let him touch me. I knew if he did, I'd melt into him and he would know he had me.

We continued this dance until my back hit the wall behind me. There was nowhere for me to go. I was trapped.

"There's no point denying the obvious," he said, leaning his head forward. "Even I can admit should I find you in any position with anyone else, I would turn them into nothing more than bloody ribbons." He caressed my cheek, exactly where Diego had sliced into my skin, and I released a small, pathetic whimper.

He blinked suddenly and leaned back, looking surprised he'd admitted it out loud.

However, he didn't back away, or give me the space I so desperately craved.

"Why are you here?" he asked in a low voice, his thumb tracing my bottom lip, causing a shudder to rip down my spine.

"I…" My eyes dropped to his lips. Suddenly, I forgot why I was here in the first place. All reason left me, and I was left with the ridiculous feeling of desire at being in Adrian's presence once more. "I wanted to tell you something."

Without warning, Adrian lunged for me. His lips claimed mine once again, just as he had in the square when he was trying to mask our presence from Patrol. This time, I wrapped my arms around him and gave in to the kiss almost immediately. My fingers went to his hair, my mouth immediately opened for him, and I arched my back, pressing myself against his body.

His tongue penetrated my mouth, tasting me, teasing me. His hard body was taut against mine, which was currently boneless and submitting to his every touch. One of his hands held my face firmly, the other cradled my hip in a possessive grasp I couldn't even fathom escaping from.

He tried to pull back, probably to give me air, but I refused. If I died, let me go this way. I wanted to kiss him, I had wanted it for so long…

His teeth nipped at my bottom lip, and he sucked it into his mouth, pressing his pelvis against my own so I could feel just how much he desired me. My groin throbbed and ached with a need I didn't understand, but I knew it was for him.

I pulled away, breathless, leaning my head back against the wall behind me. Through half-mast lids, I tried to read him, tried to understand what the kiss was for.

"I have been wanting to do that since the last time I kissed you, Hannah Walker," he murmured. His fingers gently pushed my chin, giving him more access to my throat.

I closed my eyes, wrapping my arms around his shoulders. His lips found my throat and my body responded in the throes of desire.

"I know what I do to you," he whispered against her skin. "Your pulse jumps out of time, telling me you belong to me. Every part of you is mine. Do you understand? You've had my blood. No one has had my blood before. No one."

"Adrian," I breathed out through a moan. "I…"

He grunted, sucking on the soft flesh of my neck.

"I need…"

He finally pulled away. His eyes were midnight blue, and the stark desire in them made me shudder. I would give him anything, I realized. I would ruin myself for him in this instant if he would only look at me like this, kiss me as he had.

I shook my head. I needed to get a grip on myself. My magick buzzed inside of me as if I'd drunk too much wine.

"Adrian," I said, stopping him before he could kiss me again.

He tilted his head to the side, looking at me silently.

"I went to see Brendan Pickard," I managed to say, even though I was out of breath. "I need to tell you what I discovered. About your girls. I want to help you."

CHAPTER NINE

Hannah

"You…wish to help *me*?" Adrian's lips tugged into a skeptical frown and his icy blue eyes regarded me with mild curiosity. "Let us retire to my office where we can discuss things more privately." I followed him up the staircase until we reached a door. He pulled me inside and tucked the door shut behind me. "You claim you wish to help? And why would you wish to align yourself with me? You know what I am. Or have you forgotten my blood runs through your veins now?" He reached up and traced the line of my throat as if to emphasize his point.

I tried and failed to suppress a shiver and his lips curved upward, a ghost of a smile on his chiseled face. He knew how he affected me and it amused him.

I scowled and pulled away from him. Perhaps this wasn't such a good idea. Being near him compromised my judgment, causing me to behave in a more wanton way than I ever expected I could. I couldn't let myself lose control again.

"Where are you going?" he murmured as his haunting gaze followed me.

"I…this was a foolish idea," I managed to get out. I needed to get to the door, get away from him before I did something I'd regret.

"No." He moved so quickly, I didn't see him until he was already positioned in front of the door—the only way out. I pulled back, afraid to make any sort of physical contact with him. "Don't run off like a scared lamb. You have no reason to fear me and you know it.

Why do you wish to help me, Hannah? Tell me. I will not suffer games."

"Games?" I said before I could stop myself. I didn't want to argue with him or fight. But I wasn't going to let him insult me. "I'm not playing games."

"I wish I had your magick," he murmured. "I wish I knew whether to believe your delectable tongue." He averted his stare from my mouth and released me from his spell. Wait, did Blood Mages even possess magick? All I knew was whenever Adrian looked at me the way he looked at me currently, it was difficult for me to do much of anything. He must have *some* form of mystical power...

"I came to you for help last night and you were very clear you wanted nothing to do with me. Why the sudden change of heart?" Adrian's words catapulted me out of my daydream.

It was a fair question. "In truth, I didn't want to," I admitted. "However, after letting your story sink in, I wanted to see if there was a truth to it."

"Why would I lie to you, knowing you'd be able to tell?" Adrian asked. He seemed genuinely curious.

I lifted a shoulder in a careless shrug. "I don't know why people choose to do the things they do," I said. "Just because you believe something is true doesn't mean it is."

"And you found confirmation with Lieutenant Pickard?" Adrian asked slowly, arching a cool brow.

I sighed. It sounded a lot crazier than it needed to be, but he had a right to question me. I paced slowly down the length of his office. Adrian's eyes were on me—nothing escaped him.

"In a way," I said. I laced my fingers behind my back. "We discussed the girl who used to work for you. Not Claire, but the one Jonathan Nyx is blamed for. A witness told Brendan she saw the dead girl help three other girls into the ocean. The second their legs touched the water, they grew tails and disappeared under the water, never to emerge. That was on your orders, wasn't it? She was doing what you told her to do."

He grunted. Instead of answering, he focused on something else. "I don't like to hear you address another man so familiarly by his first name," he said.

For a moment, I paused my pacing, trying to figure out what he meant. Only then did I realize who he was speaking about. "Brendan?" I asked, the word coming out in a swell of disbelief. "You can't possibly think I harbor feelings for him when it's my sister who loved him, and he, her."

"I don't care," Adrian said. His voice was firm, and his eyes darkened.

"I've just told you about a witness who saw girls turn into mermaids and all you care about is me addressing a man by his first name?"

Adrian said nothing in return but crossed his arms across his chest. I guessed he'd already said what he wanted to say.

I blew out a breath and looked away, playing with the ends of my hair. I didn't like the possessive glint in his eyes as he regarded me. I especially didn't like the pull in my groin in response.

"Look," I said, trying again. "I want to help, but if you'd rather I didn't, I can go. I only wanted to tell you what I heard. What you do with the information is up to you."

"I will gladly accept your help, Hannah Walker," Adrian said. "This witness your friend mentioned, do they have a name? Someone we can question ourselves?"

I shook my head. "I didn't think to ask him," I said. I felt rather foolish at not doing so. "I wanted to come and tell you as quickly as I could. I wanted to…"

Make sure you were safe.

Of course, I didn't tell him that. But perhaps I could find out.

"I can go back and ask Brendan—" I offered.

"I'd prefer you didn't," Adrian said tersely. "We'll find out another way. Perhaps I can do some digging and discover the identity myself. What doesn't make sense is the fact they claim they saw the girl guide the three Sirens into the sea."

I crossed my arms over my chest. "Why would that not make sense?" I asked.

"Because my deliveries come directly from Underedge," he said. "I wait in a location near the docks, and they emerge from the water. They don't go into it. Perhaps the witness was watching as my employee released the girls I'd freed back into the water. That seems more feasible."

"Whoever is rescuing the Sirens must know they're Sirens," I said. "That's why they're being led back to the water rather than somewhere on land."

I dropped into the chair directly in front of Adrian's desk. Unfortunately, he was right. At least, his theory was sound. I remembered Adrian insisting on having a plan to try to free those he could. I hadn't wanted to acknowledge someone could do something both so initially wretched and then do something so selfless.

"So, I came here for nothing," I said, fiddling with the skirts of my dress.

"How you wound me," he murmured, placing his hand over his heart. "And here I thought you were finally coming to like me."

I pressed my lips together, observing him the way prey might watch a predator. I wasn't sure what to say, so I said nothing. His words were soft and silky, flattering in all the right ways.

But they had to be lies.

Adrian Blood was not the sort of man who wanted anything to do with love. And I— I felt something for him, though I couldn't be sure if love described it. I hoped not; I had no desire to have my heart broken, as Lizzie had.

She'd had to pick up the pieces of her heart once she and Brendan's betrothal ended. And then there was my failed relationship with Henry, which had caused me stress. Relationships didn't seem to work in my family.

"You're thinking again," he said, his gaze focused.

"I am," I admitted, pushing my feelings firmly down inside.

"Tell me," he commanded.

I looked up at him, feeling his eyes on me, filled with intrigue and something else. I flexed my fingers, rolled them into a fist, and flexed them again.

"I don't understand you," I admitted, shaking my head. "You dare to claim me, to tell me you don't like the prospect of me visiting other men, and yet you don't speak of possessing any sort of emotion for me other than something physical. You treat me as if I belong to you, as property."

"Emotion?" he asked. "You think it's easy for someone like me to show emotion? I was created by people who had an agenda." He scoffed. "I wasn't held by my mother when I cried or educated by my father. I have no relations save for the ones I need or can use. Physical release, food, business interactions. These don't require emotion. I don't require it to guarantee my survival. Such a thing would make me weak and vulnerable."

"I disagree," I said, dropping my hand and looking at him over my shoulder. He was much closer than I anticipated. "It's your ignorance that makes you weak. Not your emotions."

"Ignorance?" He smirked, cocking his head to the side. "You think I'm ignorant?"

"You admitted to such a thing," I pointed out.

He barked out a laugh, and I wasn't sure whether I wanted to fall into the sound or run from it.

"And when, pray tell, did I do that?" he asked.

"You said you're unfamiliar with emotions based on the reason for your conception and how you were raised to be," I said. "Which means you have little experience with emotions. This means what you are feeling, you can't label because you don't know what it is. That ignorance makes you weak. If you knew what you felt, you'd be able to do something about it."

Before I could say anything further, Adrian lunged for me. My back hit the wall behind me, startling me, but his hands on my waist kept me steady. His mouth latched onto mine, forcing it to mold to his with the swipe of his tongue. If he could devour me, consume my heart and soul, I think he would have.

"And what do I feel for you, Hannah Walker?" he asked huskily when he pulled away. But he didn't go far. "Desire? Possession?" He traced the column of my throat with his finger, and I tilted my head to the side, giving him better access. "Or perhaps I'm using you because a relationship with you would benefit me."

His words hit me like a slap in the face. I blinked my eyes open and stared at him, trying to gauge the truth of his words without using my magick on him. I didn't want to violate his trust even if a selfish part of me yearned for just that. Because it would make sense. I was set to take over my father's business. And if I took over his business, I would have power over his fees, over the protection his business earned with each fee. Getting close to me was akin to getting close to my father because he could use me to manipulate my father.

My eyes burned..

"Perhaps you're right," I said. "Maybe I'm nothing but some toy to play with. Thank you, Mr. Blood, for being so honest about your feelings. I assure you I'll never contact you again unless it's a *very necessary* business matter."

I dropped my shoulders, refusing to cry. My chest seized with pain, and every beat it took was as if it were stabbing itself. I didn't want to cry; he mustn't know how much he affected me.

I strode toward the door of the officel, but his bulk blocked me yet again. I blew out a frustrated breath and stomped my foot like a petulant child.

"What do you want with me?" Suddenly, I didn't care I was supposed to be afraid of him. I just wanted to go home and sleep.

Adrian was silent for a long moment. His eyes were on my face, taking me in. What he expected to see, I didn't know, but I remained still.

"You leave me…unsettled," he finally said. This seemed like a huge burden for him to admit, so I said nothing, wanting to see if he needed to say more. "Sometimes, I find myself drawn to you like a moth to a flame. Other times, I need to keep away from you lest I fall into your trap."

"What trap?" I asked, genuinely confused. "If you think I'm trying to ensnare you—"

"I don't think you're trying at all, which makes it all the worse." He clamped his teeth down, and with utter fascination, I watched as his incisors elongated.

My heart skipped a beat at the sight. I was afraid, but I was also…intrigued. Before I could stop myself, I reached out and used the pad of my finger to brush the point of his fang.

A low moan from him filled the room, and my face flushed. I yanked my hand away from him, as though I'd been bitten.

Adrian grabbed my wrist, however. "Don't go," he whispered, bringing my fingers back to his mouth, his teeth…

A scream interrupted us and suddenly, the brothel was in a tizzy. The commotion could be heard outside, but I had no idea what was going on.

Adrian cocked his head in curiosity, and I assumed his special hearing heard something I didn't. He locked eyes with me.

"It's a raid," he said grimly.

CHAPTER TEN

Hannah

Adrian didn't even hesitate.

He wrapped his arms around me, tossed me over his shoulder as I uttered a mortified squeak, and got me unseen out of the lobby and into some sort of secret office I doubted anyone knew about. As much as I detested what he was, there were perks I couldn't deny. The speed that he employed just now couldn't be witnessed by a human eye. Even though I didn't know much, if anything, about Blood Mages, I was sure others like Adrian would have difficulty picking it up. In other words, no one knew where we were.

Once we were tucked inside, he snapped his fingers and candles illuminated the small room so we could see. Besides a desk and a chair, there was little else. It was adjacent to the main office, but used as a safe haven just in case, for moments such as this one.

"You can speak freely," he said. "They won't hear us."

I looked into his icy blue eyes. There were so many questions I wanted to ask with no idea where to start. Part of me was scared of him, not because he'd hurt me—somehow, I knew he wouldn't—but of what he was capable of.

"I see the fear in your eyes," he stated, his voice emotionless. I didn't deny his claim. He nodded once, almost approvingly. "Good. You need to remember what I am to you, and you can't partake in some fantasy where I'm human."

I didn't know what to say.

"Because I'm not," he continued. "I never will be. This is who I've always been, what I was created to be. Anything else, any hope for a different life, is foolish."

"I thought…I didn't realize Blood Mages had magick," I managed to say. I was winded still from our escape. He took me by surprise by offering me a chair to sit on. Part of me wanted to refuse, but I wound up taking a seat, regardless of what my pride wanted. "I mean, I heard the rumors, the compulsion, but…"

"Why do you think we're called Mages?" he asked. "For someone with your brilliance, you know nothing of my world."

I looked down at my fingers. He was right, of course. I thought I knew much, but I was ignorant of the reality of my environment.

"Then teach me," I said in a soft voice.

Adrian raised his brows. I lifted my face to look at him, determination flaring through my body. I wouldn't cower this time.

"Teach me the real world," I said. "I've been sheltered my entire life. I barely know a thing about my magick. You know more." I lifted a hand to gesture at him. "You could help me figure out the truth of everything. Why does everyone feel threatened by Jonathan Nyx? What released him just before his Consumption? What happened to my mother, my aunt?"

"You think I know all?" He snorted, shaking his head. I was surprised such a sound would come from someone like him. "And what I do know, I wouldn't tell you because it only puts you at greater risk. And I will never risk *you*, Hannah." His eyes caught mine and the intensity behind his gaze caused my heart to skip a beat. Color warmed my face and I tried to look away but I couldn't. Mercifully, he looked away and released me from it a moment later.

"Do you hear what's going on down there? My brothel is being raided by Patrol. Never has that happened before."

I tilted my head. I heard screams then silence. "Who would do such a thing?" I asked. "Who would have Patrol raid your brothel?"

"Someone with power," Adrian said grimly. "Perhaps it's Lieutenant Pickard and that drunk, blubbering Lead of his who looks at one as if you're the cause of all his problems. All I know is this has never happened before. There's a reason I'm paying your father. He knows everything that's going on. There should be no justification for this raid."

Another scream pierced the silence.

"We should help," I said, making my way to the door. "It's not fair we're here and—"

Adrian whooshed by me, positioning himself once more in front of the door. "We won't go anywhere," he said in a low, firm voice that brokered no room for argument. "I told you I will not risk you."

"But your girls—"

"The only girl I possess is you," he said. The words shocked me and I didn't like the way they curled warmly around my body, didn't like the way my pelvis pulsated at the clear possession in his tone. "I couldn't care less about the others."

"I'm the only one in possession of myself," I snapped before I could stop myself. "No one owns me. I'm not someone's property."

"You *are* mine, Hannah Walker." Adrian's eyes flashed. "I have already told you as much."

"But the Pascals," I said. When had my mouth suddenly gone dry? I tried to swallow so when I spoke again, there wouldn't be this rough, raw sound that came out. "I know they've threatened you in some way. I know—"

"I don't care about the Pascals," he said through gritted teeth.

I flinched at his tone and took a step back. I didn't think he would hurt me, but I needed space from him. I needed to know I was still in control of my actions, even if we were trapped here.

"You are my weakness," Adrian said, eyes narrowed. I couldn't tell if he was angry at me or the situation occurring in his place of business. A bit of both probably. "And normally I slaughter any weakness I find myself drawn to." He reached for my face, cupping my cheek. "I watch as the life disappears from their eyes. As they choke on their blood. And then I celebrate I never have to concern myself with them at all."

I was too afraid to speak, too afraid to breathe. Even when his thumb began to caress my bottom lip, even when he dropped his gaze and stared intently at my mouth, I found I couldn't move. I didn't think I wanted to.

"What are you thinking?" he murmured, his voice silky as what I imagined a lover's caress might feel like. "What is going through that head of yours, Hannah Walker?"

"You've had weaknesses like me before?" I finally asked.

His lips curved into a smug smile and he leaned closer to me. For a brief moment, I was certain he was going to kiss me again. I was ready to push up onto my toes so I could easily reach him.

"Is that what troubles you?" he asked. "You believe you're not the first who has bewitched me so? I'm sorry to break this to you, Hannah, but not all weaknesses come in such alluring packages as you. Sometimes, they are merely acquaintances. Friends, even. Used against me, my weakness becomes an enemy, and it is only to release them from suffering when I must kill them."

"Who would do such a thing?" I asked before I could stop myself. "And why?"

"Compliance is not so easily wrought from me," he murmured, looking down. He didn't release my cheek, however, and I didn't pull away. "I worry you will be my downfall. Perhaps it is best if we don't work together."

"I thought you wanted that?" I said, trying to keep the tremble from my voice. Was he pushing me away, saying he wanted nothing more to do with me? "I thought I could help—"

"Foolish girl," he said, interrupting me. "I want much more than your help. I want to claim every inch of your body so you fully belong to me. I never want to be parted from you because I can't trust anyone else to keep you safe the way I can. I want to feast from you, taste you in a way no one ever could. You should fear me, Hannah Walker, and yet you tantalize me, you tease me, by coming to this lion's den alone under the guise of help. You lecture me about emotions, and yet you tell me nothing of yours. What am I supposed to do with you?"

"Why?" I asked. The word squeaked past my pressed lips, and color immediately filled my cheeks.

"Why?" he asked, repeating my question with a hint of surprise.

"Yes, why me?" I leaned into the question, deciding not to run from it. There was just as much danger in here as there was out there, and I realized I had to stop running from it. I had to face it.

His lips curved up as his eyes darkened.

"Simple," he murmured, leaning so close to me his lips were almost grazing my jawline, "I want you to feel the same way, to beg me for what you need from me. I want to hear the pleading in your voice and know you want me of your own free will. I would never force myself upon you. And you *will* beg, Hannah."

"How could you possibly know?" I asked, trying to control my words so they wouldn't tremble.

"I can feel it in your kiss how you hunger for me." His lips pressed against my jawline this time, an unexpectedly chaste kiss as soft as a butterfly's wing. "How you wish to explore your ignorance of what pleasure is."

I pulled away from him, trying to read him. I didn't understand what he meant. How was I ignorant?

"You claim *my* ignorance lies in my lack of experience with emotions," he said. "And yours lies in your lack of experience with your body. Tell me, have you pleasured yourself before?"

Before I could stop it, I slapped him across the face. I was certain the blush staining my features was blotchy and uncouth, but I couldn't control it. How dare he talk to me so boldly over something he had no business knowing about?

"I'm guessing not," Adrian said, undeterred by the slap. He lifted his hand to rub his face and leaned down. "Probably because you are unfamiliar with your body and the pleasure you can bring to yourself. Would you like me to teach you?"

"Stop it," I whispered, my voice a pathetic sound of air and breath. In the tense air between us, below I heard a commotion and people shouting. What on earth was happening?

"I can, you know." He took the hand that slapped him and yanked me to him. One hand found my waist, holding me in position, while the other cupped my cheek and tilted my head back so I was forced to look him in the eyes. The noise below disappeared as I struggled to resist him. "I can teach you all about pleasure. I can bring you to your knees. I can make you beg me for more—and I would give it." He cocked his head and frowned. "What the devil is going on down below? It sounds like some of my patrons are getting rowdy. Too much rum I expect."

"I am a respectable woman," I managed to get out. "My virtue is for the man I marry and no one else."

"Who said anything about claiming your virtue?" Adrian asked, arching a brow. His lips turned up. "There are ways to pleasure that don't require connection the way you know it. I know how badly you wish to control your magick. And yet, how can you control something you know so little about? You know nothing of your body. Nothing of what makes you, you." His eyes searched mine, suddenly serious. "Do you even know what you want from the life you have?"

In truth, I hadn't thought about it. My life had been planned for me since Mother died, and even more, once Father deemed Lizzie unfit to run his business. Lizzie ascertained freedom I never had. I liked the relationship I had with my father. I liked that he depended on me, trusted me, in a way he never would with her.

But I found I also longed for Lizzie's freedom to discover what I wanted for myself and not because I wanted to please someone else.

"Why not take what you want from me and be done with it?" I asked. "I've heard the rumors. I know pillaging is something associated with Blood Mages. Why don't you partake in such violence?"

"Because it is much more satisfying when you're begging me for it," he said. "I will never hurt you, Hannah. You saved my life multiple times. You risked everything to come to me tonight even though you know what I am."

"You ask me what I want," I said. "I want to help find the girls. If I can prove the Pascals are behind this, perhaps war will be averted. Perhaps it will force Diego to break his betrothal with Everly."

And perhaps it would guarantee Adrian's safety from them.

Of course, I didn't tell him this. Let him think whatever he wanted.

Before he could respond to me, deathly silence filled the air. It was eerie, and uncouth, as if everyone who'd been noisy below us had suddenly lost their voices…or worse.

CHAPTER ELEVEN

Adrian

"We should go see what happened. Something isn't right." Hannah's quiet voice filled the space of the office.

I lifted one eye brow, surprised she would suggest that, when her heartbeat echoed in my ear, as hard and as fast as a baby hummingbird.

"I'm sure everything is fine. Just a couple of fights broke out, no doubt. The doormen will take care of it. It's why I pay them," I told her. Was she trying to get away from me, or was she genuinely concerned about what might have happened to my business?

Foolish mortal. If anything *was* wrong downstairs, I didn't want her being caught in the middle of it.

She could be discovered here by Patrol and when rumors spread through Ankura the way sightings of Jonathan Nyx did, it wouldn't be long before word got back to her father. I was certain Reginald Walker wouldn't want people to view Hannah as scandalous, especially since Lizzie was already deemed "abnormal" for a woman of her society as it was. Should he have two odd daughters, things wouldn't be good for him. He might be viewed as less than worthy of his position of port manager, despite he and the governor being tied by family bonds.

And yet, Hannah didn't seem to care about any of that. She was willing to risk everything to ensure strangers were safe and protected.

My nostrils flared. I couldn't have anything happen to her, especially not now she'd agreed to help me figure out what had happened to my shipment of girls. I needed her safe and protected.

"I never took you for a coward, Adrian Blood," she said softly.

"*What* did you just call me?" I demanded angrily.

No one, not even you, calls me a coward.

I thought she'd flinch, cower beneath my scathing tone but she continued to hold my gaze. Grudging respect bubbled up in my chest. I forced myself to ignore it, not wanting to give her any sort of credit for standing up to me, for not being afraid. I needed her to remember what I was: a monster. Someone she shouldn't trust. She should fear me as if I was living proof nightmares existed within her reality.

Yet I couldn't help but hope she saw me as something else too, and the conflict between needing to be both monster and lover caused me great confusion. I wanted her terribly, but knew, deep down, she could never be mine, which made me want to push her away. I couldn't seem to lean into either decision fully, leaving me a contradictory mess.

"A c-coward," she said, stumbling over the word.

The look of trepidation on her face tempered my ire and I bit back a smile, feeling my gaze soften as I took her in. I had the sudden urge to take her into my arms, press her against my chest, and bury my face in her hair. Wrinkling my nose, I turned from her. I didn't want to feel this way.

"What you don't seem to realize, darling, is by going down the stairs we reveal our presence within the building. If the law is downstairs, and the disturbance *was* a raid, they would see you here. With me," I said nonchalantly.

I couldn't let her think it was a good idea to leave the safety of this room. Not when I needed her to help me track my missing Sirens. If she wanted to expose herself after that was settled, so be it. I had no control over her. The stubborn fool would do as she pleased.

I rolled my shoulders back, easing the stiffness in them.

She continued to stare up at me with those forest green eyes. Even though her fear of me was palpable, she didn't back down. She didn't want to be afraid of me, but she couldn't deny she was.

I realized, then, I didn't want her fear. I wanted something else.

"Adrian, these are your people," she said, tucking a stray strand of hair behind her ear and looking at the ground. "They rely on you for protection the same way you rely on my father."

I growled, bristling. "I rely on your father for nothing," I corrected tightly. "I'm forced to play this game he has where businesses pay him a fee, but he protects nothing."

She flinched at my words. *Good.*

Sometimes, it felt as though Hannah had all the evidence in the world in regards to the cruelty and manipulation of her father, of what he could truly be, but she ignored it. At the same time, she could look at *me* like I was some sort of monster, someone who made choices based on my own needs and wants without considering anyone else.

I was selfish. I didn't deny that. But to pretend as though her father wasn't was foolish. I expected better from her.

"Fine," she said. Her chin jutted out defiantly, gaze clashing with mine. "You aren't like my father. But your people still expect *your* protection, and that's fair. They work here for you, don't they? You house them, you feed them, you pay them."

"Fair?" The word fell out of my mouth and my lips curved into a grin. "Where in the world does fair fit into your life? Granted, you were born with a silver spoon hanging out of your mouth so you know nothing of this world you live in, but I don't owe them anything."

"You don't believe that." I didn't like how sure her words were, like she truly believed what she spewed.

"Excuse me?"

Where was this girl coming from? The last time I'd seen this spunk was the night we'd studied her friend's body. The night we first kissed. I didn't want to think about that night. There were too many…feelings I hadn't sorted through just yet.

"You don't believe that," she repeated. "If you did, you wouldn't go out of your way to find your missing girls."

"Foolish mortal," I said, chuckling. I brushed past her, careful to touch her just barely. "I'm looking for them because if I don't, the Pascals will have my head."

Or they'll do something terrible to you.

I couldn't add the last part. Not because I didn't want to scare her but because I didn't want to admit it to her. She made me vulnerable, and fool I was, I'd made it obvious to Diego Pascal. I should have known better, but I'd been too consumed trying to figure out who wanted to kill me, and then discovering Pepper was behind it—the one Mage I trusted with everything— had been enough to distract me.

"Perhaps *they* called a raid on purpose," she suggested.

Yes, Diego Pascal knew I had a weakness and had no problem exploiting it. I wanted to kill him myself but I knew I couldn't—yet. Even Hannah…a dark part of me wanted to rid myself of her completely so she wouldn't be able to hold this over me. I would not be bound to her any longer. I could be free.

"Think about it," I forced myself to say. "If the Sirens go missing, the Pascals will simply blame me for it. I'm replaceable. This business is not. Raiding it, potentially discovering the truth of what's being done here…" I shook my head. "It doesn't make sense for this to be them." I paced around the room. "And it doesn't make sense you, yourself, would care. You threaten your life simply by allying yourself with me. Do you forget what I am? Shall I remind you? You had no problem turning your back on me back in your room after your sister's appearance. I would rather you stop with this facade."

"You came to me for help," she bit back. Any lingering fear seemed to completely vanish from her tone. "Or do you not remember that visit?"

"I remember," I said, taking a step toward her. I should hate her fear was gone, that she didn't give me the respect I thought I deserved, but something in me flipped at the thought she wasn't afraid of me. "I remember losing my sanity for a moment. Why would I ever think to ask you, especially when you're consumed by your magick? You realize our kind is more similar than different. Your magick, especially untapped, uncontrolled magick, is just as dangerous as mine. If I'm a monster, Hannah Walker, you're one too. You just wear a pretty mask and hide yourself away. But you're just the same as I am."

"Don't you think I realize that?" she whispered. "Pushing you away meant I didn't need to be confronted with the fact I have no idea who I am anymore. Am I the genteel young daughter of a respectable man? Or am I a witch, ready to be Consumed by those I once considered my friends should they ever discover the truth? I can't...I can't risk anything happening to you. And if we are together in any capacity, there is a risk." She looked at me, really looked at me. It took everything in me not to flinch at the direct gaze. "Adrian, the Pascals are looking for any excuse to cause you harm. When I did what I did to Pepper, I didn't intend—"

"I know," I said in a low voice. I locked eyes with her unexpectedly. Hers were glassy, unsure like she wanted to cry but couldn't.

I nearly took a step back from her even though I reveled in her presence. The last thing I wanted was to deal with a crying mortal. Tears were the worst sorts of weapons. I wasn't sure how to defend myself from them. I saw them as a weakness, as something that made me uncertain and uncomfortable. Under normal circumstances, I would end the tears by cutting off life or removing myself from the situation. As it was, I could do neither of those things with Hannah, even if my first instinct was to flee.

"You...you do?" Her voice cracked, and it felt as though my heart cracked along with it.

"You are no murderer, Hannah," I said. How did she not understand? "You reacted. Nothing could be done otherwise."

"You're saying I'm not in control of myself," she said.

"You're not," I pointed out. "I say this not to insult you but to remind you you're human. Despite the magick that flows through you, you are an imperfect being. You are still learning. And Pepper occurred because you were protecting me. You can't think of yourself as a monster for protecting someone you care about."

"But you said—"

"I know what I said." I immediately softened my harsh tone, and internally admonished myself for caring in the first place. "You think of yourself as someone who wielded a deadly weapon and used force. It's why you avoid me, fear. You know I won't harm you and yet you fear your feelings for me. What you would do for me."

She said nothing to deny it. Good. That was a start.

"What do you suggest we do about this?" I asked instead.

She let out a shaky breath. "I think we need to go down and check on the situation," she said after a moment. "Maybe there are clues as to who's behind it if you don't think it's the Pascals. We need to stabilize the situation."

"And us?" Adrian asked.

Hannah finally met my eyes. "There is no us," she said, brushing hair from her face. "There never was. We both know we want different things. We come from different places." She rubbed her lips together. "You're not wrong, though. There is something I feel for you...but I shouldn't. I could never expect you to bind yourself to me and I won't accept anything less."

Her words struck me in a way her magick never could. I was surprised she was able to speak so freely. I doubted I could do the same.

She stepped away from the wall and crossed the room.

"Where are you going?" I asked.

She stopped when she reached the door and looked over her shoulder. "I'm going to see if anyone needs help," she said. "And then I'm going home to sleep. I'm exhausted."

"Then return home now," I insisted. "I will walk you there myself."

"I would prefer it if you didn't," she said, twisting the handle.

"Why not?" I demanded.

"It will be easier to rid myself of you if you weren't around me longer than you needed to be," she said softly, almost regrettably. "The worst possible pain is a lingering hope that won't let me be. I will help you, Adrian. But beyond that, we should part. Not because you're a monster. Not because I am. But because it would be much too dangerous for us to be together." Before I could stop her, she walked out of the room.

CHAPTER TWELVE

Hannah

The second I reached the bottom of the stairs, I was smothered in magick. It lingered in the air like foul smoke from a burning fire. Something bad had certainly happened. The metallic scent of blood filled the air.

"What happened?" I asked.

"Men came here, searching for something," one of the Sirens said. "They...they broke everything. They never said what they were looking for...but...but..."

"But?" Adrian pushed.

"Something seemed off about them." She glanced down at her shoulder where she brushed glass from the clothing. There was a tear in the thin material. "Like...like they weren't in control of themselves. Like they were acting in a way that represented someone else."

"Like they were controlled by magick?" I asked in a low voice.

My mind raced with possibilities. Unless the Pascals knew someone who'd willingly use magick to intimidate Adrian, it appeared more and more likely someone else was responsible for whatever had happened.

The only people I knew with magick were my sister, my cousins, and my aunt and her coven. I doubted my cousins knew about Adrian Blood, and while Lizzie didn't like him, I was certain she wouldn't call a raid and draw attention to her magick.

Which left Aunt Thaya. Though why would she care about Adrian? Why would she risk exposing herself and her fellow witches by coming here and causing havoc?

I couldn't think about this now, not until the people who worked for Adrian were taken care of.

I walked over to the girl I'd seen him talk to on the stairs, the one who'd been the cause of my jealousy and the shattered glass. It felt so long ago. Had it only been hours?

Suddenly someone's fingers wrapped around my wrist. "Where are you going?" Adrian demanded in his low, rough voice.

I shot him an annoyed look. "You have people bleeding and bruised thanks to this raid. I'm going to help them get cleaned up."

"You can...heal?" he asked, tilting his head to the side.

"I didn't say..." I shook my head, ignoring the way his fingers still lingered on my wrist. "I can't heal. But I can stitch a bit. Lizzie's had her fair share of injuries and I was forced to learn how to clean and dress them so Father wouldn't notice and scold her for being so rambunctious." I perked my brow. "You should help too. They're your employees. They wouldn't be here if it weren't for you."

Adrian's jaw ticked. He looked as though he had more to say on the matter, but decided ultimately not to say anything, something I was grateful for. I didn't wish to argue with him if I could help it. Right now, I needed to distract myself. I didn't even want to analyze what had taken place between us.

"What do you expect me to do?" he asked. "Feed everyone my blood so they can heal?"

I wrinkled my nose at the thought of anyone else tasting Adrian's blood. I didn't like the possessiveness that clawed at my insides, but I ignored it for the time being. Right now, I needed to focus on the task at hand, offering assistance to those who needed it.

"Answer me." His words developed a dark taint to them, one that struck me deep inside, stroking the fire that simmered within my very core. "Would you want that?"

He was goading me, wanting some sort of reaction but I refrained. "The look on your face is full of distaste," he said. "Tell me, would you ask me to do that? Everyone would heal, just as you want them to. Everyone would—"

"No," I snapped before I could stop myself.

I hated he was able to get under my skin. I curled my fingers until they made fists, digging my nails in my palms. The last thing I wanted to do was stroke Adrian Blood's already astronomical ego.

"Why not, Hannah?" he asked, dipping his head and leaning in close.

Too close.

The thought of Adrian touching me jolted me out of my thoughts. I couldn't sit here thinking about Adrian like this, not when there was groaning and crying filling the room.

I shook my head and stepped around Adrian, making my way into the lobby. There were bodies everywhere. Some were unconscious judging by the even rise and fall of their chests. Some were silently crying, holding on to an injured body part such as a bloody arm or sliced thigh.

I walked up to the bar, trying to ignore the sight, my stomach rolling at the sharp smell of blood. I searched for the bartender, sure they'd be able to assist.

He was cowering behind the bar.

"You," I said. "I need you."

The bartender looked at me. "What do you want?" he asked in a shaking voice. He seemed human and I couldn't blame him for his fear. I had magick to protect me and I could only imagine how he felt.

"I need as many dish rags as you have, a bottle of rum, and some bandages, if you have them on hand," I said. I hoped my voice didn't tremble as I focused on going through a list in my head. "And a bowl of water." As an afterthought, I added, "Please."

The bartender looked at me before nodding once. He sprang into action. I sighed in relief and turned to look at the damage. The brothel itself would have to be closed for a few days at least until the place was once again suitable for clients. With glass shattered everywhere, broken furniture, injured girls, and a frustrated Blood Mage, I wasn't sure when that would be. Adrian's business was going to suffer and I wondered whether that had been the point of the raid.

I leaned against the bar, following this train of thought. *Why* did this raid happen? My father protected the brothel, so there shouldn't have been one in the first place. Which meant someone with power had sent Patrol to attack it. Or...*no*. Not Patrol. There was evidence of magick here. Which could mean other Blood Mages with surprise magick, or witches. I wondered if Lizzie knew anything. I could always go to Aunt Thaya, but she didn't like Adrian and probably wouldn't care. If anything, she'd likely be happy this had happened in the first place.

I sighed, wondering where the bartender had gotten to. Why would Aunt Thaya risk exposure? Adrian knew where she was. And if he believed she was behind this, he'd certainly want to find her for revenge.

Perhaps it had been the Pascals after all. They'd sent him a warning before—could this be another?

It didn't feel right, though, especially after Adrian's logic on the subject. The Pascals cared about this business and the money they profited from. Whether it was the Blood Mages as clientele or something else entirely, the Pascals had no problem risking Adrian himself because he could be replaced. He'd said as much when we were in his private office.

My musing was interrupted by the bartender, who dropped the supplies I requested on the bar in front of me, with a small bowl of water as well.

"Thank you," I said, gathering everything in my arms as carefully as I could.

I began to make my way through the crowd. No one seemed to notice me or even look my way. I chewed my bottom lip, trying to figure out the best way to offer help.

"If anyone..." Groans filled the silence. I looked over my shoulder, hoping Adrian was there, hoping he might be able to help, but I couldn't see him.

I was alone. My shoulders drooped and I cast my gaze around again. I couldn't simply give up because I wasn't sure what to do. If Lizzie were here, she'd know.

But she wasn't. It was only me and I needed to step up.

I cleared my throat. "Does anyone require immediate medical assistance?" I asked loudly and stood tall, hoping to seem more assertive than I felt.

No one seemed to pay much attention to me. I tried again, much louder this time. "Does anyone require immediate medical assistance?"

"I do."

I turned and came into contact with a pair of beautiful blue eyes. My heart stuttered for a moment as I recognized her as the girl Adrian seemed taken with. A too familiar prick of doubt and jealousy thrummed through my head but I ignored it. Instead, I cleared my throat and forced myself to walk toward her. She stood holding the stair banister, pain etched on her face.

When I reached the stairs, I carefully set down the bowl of water. She was just as beautiful up close as she was far away.

"Hi," I said, trying to force a chirpiness I didn't feel. "Where is your injury? Perhaps I can help heal it. Not with magick," I asserted hastily. "With medical means."

She lifted her shirt to reveal a deep gash on her side. My eyes widened and I dropped to my knees. I took the washcloth and placed it in the water.

"I'm going to clean the wound," I announced. "This may hurt. If you'd like to sit down, I would do so now."

She nodded once and took a seat on the stairs. I carefully dabbed the rag against her bleeding wound, then grabbed another one, this time dowsing it with rum. When I pressed it against her taut form, she flinched and let out a long hiss.

"You know, I hated Adrian the second I saw his face," the woman said, taking me by surprise.

"Oh?" I wasn't sure how to respond to that, so I said nothing. I pressed the cloth into her a few more times just to ensure the wound was thoroughly cleaned.

"He's too perfect, if that makes sense," she said with a sardonic grin. "I hated him when he gave me a room. I hated him when he told me what was required of me. And I hated him even more when he was kind."

I pulled away from the woman and looked at her.

"Adrian Blood isn't a kind man but that doesn't mean he's incapable of kindness," she said. "He refused to take a shipment of girls a month ago and was punished accordingly."

"Punished?" I asked as I grabbed a bandage and pressed it into her side.

She paused as I adjusted it until it fit.

"He will never tell this to you, but he does care what you think," she said. "They killed one of the girls, you know. After he refused. As much as I want to hate him, I must admit there is nothing even he can do. His hands are tied."

CHAPTER THIRTEEN

Hannah

I couldn't get the girl's words out of my head. Adrian was trapped by someone or something into not being able to refuse what was asked of him? I finished dressing her wounds and attempted to focus on the task at hand and not the fact there was much Adrian wasn't telling me, things making him more human than he would have preferred.

"Why are you doing this, witch?"

I started at her words and snapped my gaze into her penetrating blue eyes. Her face

remained impassive.

"What?" she asked, lips curving down as I finished wrapping the bandages around her stomach. "I can scent magick. Yours surrounds you like a protective shield." She paused. "Although, I'm not sure if you're protecting yourself from others...or others from yourself." She looked around. "Do you sense the magick here? This raid was conducted by one of your kind."

I curled errant hair behind my ears and attempted to tie the bandage at her side. I needed it tight so it wouldn't fall off, but not tight where it was difficult for her to breathe. My face heated up despite the fact it was a particularly crisp night. How could she know what I was? I'd never heard of anyone being able to scent magick save for other witches. What did that even mean? Or was she trying to fish for information? I didn't know how to respond to it, so I said nothing.

"Hide your secrets if you must," she said, tossing blonde hair over her shoulders, "but if I can figure out what you are, I'm sure others will as well."

"Is that a threat?" I all but hissed. I wasn't sure where this defensiveness was coming from, but I didn't appreciate this…this harpie to think she could intimidate me. I tied the bandages a tad too tightly.

She sucked in a breath, arching a brow, almost as though she knew exactly what I was doing. "No," she replied. She seemed amused at my action. "A warning, Ms. Walker. Your father is an important figure on this island. What might happen if it was discovered not only is one daughter filled with scandal, a blacksmith shop, and a broken engagement, but his other, genteel daughter possesses magick?"

My eyes widened. I glanced around, looking over my shoulder, hoping nobody could hear her. There were many prying ears in a place like this.

"How do you know all this?" I asked in a harsh whisper, leaning toward her more closely than proper decorum dictated.

"You pick things up in a place like this," she said with a nonchalant shrug. She pulled her hair back over her shoulder and began to pull tiny strands and knot them together. "Clients like to brag. You see, Hannah, I'm not sure if you realize this just yet because you have such little experience, but men are stupid. They like to pretend they're more important than they are. Importance is associated with power and knowledge. So, to impress someone like me, they loosen their tongue and start talking about what makes them special. The truth is none of them has power. None of them is special. They think they can bestow the greatest pleasure on me, when I'm greatly unaffected by them and their prowess." She rolled her eyes. "Very few men know the female body, though I do hear Adrian Blood is among the few who gives pleasure just as much as receiving it." She looked at me from her peripheral. "Well? Will you not comment on the truth of this?"

"W-what?" I asked, my cheeks heating up again. "I wouldn't know. I don't— I'm not sure." I bristled, stepping back from her. I had done my job. I had helped her with her wounds.

The woman started laughing, a low, melodic sound like bells tinkling. "I only tease," she said. "Not about him, though. I *do* hear this. Hessie hears everything. " She touched her chest with a bloodied hand.

"I don't understand why you'd want me to know," I snapped sourly.

I didn't want to hear about Adrian with other women. I clamped my hands shut, afraid I might lose control of my magick if I felt any more anger or jealousy. Denying it would only cause my magick to bristle, to combust, and if I did that in front of these people, I would be tying my noose. Regardless of whether she believed me or not, I couldn't give her confirmation. It was too risky.

"He does care for you," she said slowly. "In his own way, of course."

I didn't want to hear that, either. What did I care if he cared for me? Without meaning to, my eyes searched for him among the crowd. I was certain he was somewhere in the lobby, probably barking orders at those capable of listening and adhering to them.

"I don't know why you're telling me any of this," I said, gathering up my supplies in my hands. "I don't care what Adrian does. He can do...whatever with whoever he pleases. It doesn't matter."

"You don't know," Hessie said. "You and Adrian haven't..." She let her voice trail off, not hiding the surprise in her words. "I thought certainly... It would make no sense for him to be this attached to you."

"He's not," I said flatly, cutting her a look. This needed to stop. Now. "The bond we have is out of obligation and nothing more. I saved his life. He's saved mine. There is no attraction, nothing that might hint at anything more."

I ignored the way he kissed me earlier.

"You're a bad liar, Hannah," Hessie said, a smile on her upturned face. "I can smell your jealousy from earlier. I know you have feelings for him, feelings you might not want but possess all the same. And he has the same feelings but is unable to recognize them for what they are. This frightens him." Her eyes sparkled with utter delight. "Don't you see? You know what you feel for him and you throw yourself into an ocean of denial. You'd rather drown in your pride than admit you love him. Because if you do that, you'd be forced to admit you love a monster. And that is not something you want."

"Stop it," I said fiercely.

"No," she snapped. "You need to know the truth. Adrian Blood is a monster. I loathe him with every fiber of my being. But he is only a cog. To stop this, I must take down the people running it."

"The Pascals?" I asked, glancing over at the water. I would have to ask the bartender to refill it with cleaner water.

"The king of Underedge himself."

I snapped my head in her direction, my eyes going wide. "Are you saying the king is responsible for what's going on?" I asked in a low voice. Suddenly, everything around me faded away—the low grunts and groans of those injured by the magick, the glass being swept up, the gentle discussion between others. None of it mattered. "The king of Underedge?"

"Do you think anything happens in his ocean without him knowing?" Hessie asked. There was a bite to her words I didn't expect and a hardness to her gaze, a twist to her lips. "He entered into a deal with the Pascals."

"But why?" I asked, leaning forward. The dirty water was forgotten. "Why would he do that to his people?"

"Why would a man do anything?" Hessie asked with a sneer. "For his own power. To expand it."

I tried to understand what she was saying. Then it dawned on me. "The war," I said. "The king is going to use the disappearance of his people as an excuse to go to war with Ankura."

"Not just Ankura, silly fool," Hessie said. "He wants Cardonia."

"And the Pascals?" I asked. "What do they have to do with this?"

She gave me a blank stare. "Certainly you can figure it out," she said. "The Pascals have more money than the Five Gods you worship. More money than anyone and anything. But money can't buy them a royal title. The only way to do that—"

"Is to marry into it," I finished, lifting my hand so my fingers barred my chin. "But Diego Pascal is engaged to my cousin, Everly."

"For now," Hessie said, lifting a shoulder. "But the king of Underedge has promised them royal titles through marriage once Cardonia and all its island towns have been taken over."

I sat back, arching my back so my posture was sufficient. The aches in my back eased with the subtle stretch.

"Underedge is going to win the war," I murmured more to myself than to her. "And they're sending Adrian's girls to feed the Blood Mages to ensure compliance with them as well."

"Blood Mages were created," Hessie said. "They'll listen to whoever provides them sex and sustenance, unfortunately. And Adrian knows this. Whatever he tells them to do, they'll listen."

"But Adrian works for the Pascals," I said.

Hessie smiled but didn't say anything. It seemed I needed to figure this information out on my own to truly understand what was going on.

"Which means the Pascals expect Adrian to comply with whatever they tell him to do," I finished. I tilted my head to the side. "Why would they expect Adrian to listen to them, though? Adrian has made his feelings about the Pascals quite clear. I doubt he would listen to them. And, in fact, as a Blood Mage, he has more power over them, right?" I blinked back at her, hoping I was understanding this correctly. "Couldn't he kill them if he wanted to?"

"If your mother was the most wicked person alive, would you still have the stomach to kill her?" Hessie asked.

I started to wring out the water that still soaked the rag. "What are you saying?" I asked. "What does my mother have anything to do with the Pascals and Adrian?"

"Perhaps not your mother." She smirked. "Perhaps someone else with magickal abilities similar to your own."

"I don't understand."

"You are smarter than this," Hessie said, shaking her head. She pursed her lips together. "Can I ask you something? Why are you here? Why are you helping us? I know what you can do. I know what you risk in terms of exposure. It's not for Adrian because I know he couldn't care less about fixing us up. So, why are you doing it?"

"Do you really think I base my actions on what he wants me to do?" I asked, almost offended.

"I know someone who used to be like you, Hannah," Hessie said. Her voice had gone surprisingly quiet, and she began to peel off the polish that adorned her fingernails. "Someone who complied with wishes to make others happy. She, too, was a fool."

"What happened to her?" I asked, my curiosity getting the better of me. I didn't even care she insulted me.

"She got hurt," Hessie said, lips tightening. "Betrayed by someone she loved, someone she looked up to. And then she got harder. She got wiser. She promised she'd never allow herself to be this weak again. Never allow anyone to hurt her." She stopped scraping at her nails and looked at me. "You should do the same. Your ignorance makes you an easy target to take advantage of."

I balked. I wanted to respond, to argue, but I stopped myself. Because the truth of the matter was, she wasn't wrong. I was easy to take advantage of. My father did it, what with his assignments, with the expectations I would take over his position. Lizzie pushed me around, insisting I attend Thaya's coven training even though I wasn't particularly sure this was the best path for me and my magick. Even Adrian...

But no.

Adrian didn't take advantage of me. At least, he didn't pretend otherwise. I knew what to expect from him now I knew what he was.

"And how do I fix that?" I asked.

"For one, you stop trusting everything everyone tells you," Hessie said as though it was obvious. "Question everything from everyone. You don't have to believe it all. And don't be afraid to stand up to other people, whether it's society itself or people you care about. Because I can tell you, from personal experience, it's those closest to you who have the most power to crush you. Especially Adrian."

I stood up. "Is there anything else ailing you?" I asked.

"One other thing," she said, standing up. Her face contorted into one of pain, but she pushed through it without complaint. "You don't have to be nice to everyone, you know. You can be a little mean. It's not going to kill anyone."

"Why do you care so much about me and what I do and what I don't do?" I asked, suddenly tired. I wanted to go home, but I couldn't. Not yet. Others needed fixing up.

"Because you are more important than you realize," Hessie said. "You shatter glass, and Adrian closes his business. For you. Don't you see that? Or are you too blinded by your doubt? That's a big inhibitor to the magick inside of you, you know. When you don't trust yourself, your emotions dictate your magick. But if you trust yourself…that's magick unto itself, isn't it?"

I stared at her for a long moment. It was the first time anyone discussing magick made sense. I looked down at my palms, wondering if I could trust myself, my magick.

But before I could say anything more, she disappeared back up the stairs and I was left to find another victim to stitch up.

I still couldn't find Adrian, but that was okay. No doubt he was trying to find out who had raided his premises. I had a lot to think about after my discussion with Hessie, and the last thing I wanted was any sort of distraction. I'd finish up here, helping anyone else who needed me, then head home to think, where my thoughts were my own and there'd be no distractions.

CHAPTER FOURTEEN

Hannah

The following morning, I crept down the stairs at home, hoping to get out the door before anyone saw me. Alas, it wasn't to be.

"Where do you think you're going?" Lizzie's voice echoed flatly in the empty foyer. I froze halfway down. I'd been hoping to sneak back to Fort Crimson to see Brendan again. After everything that had happened at the brothel last night, I needed to speak to him, and ask him if anyone in his unit had magick that helped keep businesses in line, regardless of the legalities surrounding it. Perhaps they made exemptions for certain people or circumstances.

If that was the case, I wanted to know why Blood's Brothel had been raided in the first place. I twisted my fingers as I slowly turned to face my sister, who wasn't usually an early morning person. It would seem she was rising earlier and earlier, perhaps to catch me out? Well, she'd succeeded. I carried on down the stairs and was soon in the entrance.

"Um, I, uh, well, there's a farmer's market today—"

Her eyes narrowed and she placed her hand on her hip. "No," she said slowly. "There's not."

"Oh." I cleared my throat, twisting my fingers even tighter. "I thought…I guess Roseanna was mistaken."

I tried to brush past her to go to the dining room, deciding I'd have to wait now until she left for her blacksmith shop. I might as well draw a cup of coffee.

"You're still seeing him, aren't you?" she asked, sliding her hand on my forearm and giving me a gentle squeeze. The small gesture was enough to stop me. "Adrian Blood."

I opened my mouth, ready to deny it. Then I huffed wearily. If I did, Lizzie would still want some kind of explanation. She knew I wasn't acting like myself; I went out far too much and I couldn't use our father's business as an excuse. I knew she was concerned about me. Whether it was because of the war brewing between Underedge and Ankura, whether it was because I was finally starting to train with Thaya, or whether it was because of Adrian and me being romantically together, I didn't know.

But she wasn't her flighty, normal self. She was more aware. Thoughtful, even. Under other circumstances, I would have been proud of her growth. As it was, it was now interfering with what I needed to do.

"I..." I cleared my throat, but I didn't see a way out of this. "Yes." It was my only option, unfortunately. She looked at me for a long time.

"And he's who you're going to see?" she asked. I knew she knew I was lying. "You told me you weren't seeing him," she said. "Just a few days ago. When you snuck back to your room. Was that a lie? Or is it this one?" She shifted her weight. "Tell me, Hannah. I don't wish to use my magick on you, but—"

"Then don't!" I snapped.

My eyes widened at my outburst and I quickly looked away from her, tucking hair behind my ear. The truth was, I'd been waiting to have this showdown with her for a long time. Now it was here, I didn't know how to handle it. I didn't want to yell at her, I didn't want to fight. Lizzie was my only sister. But I didn't appreciate the veiled threat of her using her magick on me. I released some of the tension inside and felt now there was no stopping it from making an exit in the words I'd bottled up, which came pouring out of me. "You've already used your magick on me, so what's stopping you now, hmm?" I demanded. I didn't even care I was shouting. I was safe at home, and even if Lizzie was angry with me, I didn't think she'd tell Father I'd been out at night. "You can go off and do whatever it is you want and no one questions you because you ruined your reputation by breaking off your engagement with Brendan. You can own a blacksmith and run it without any supervision. You can use your magick on me to seek the truth from my lies without allowing me to retain anything for myself! Why? Why do *you* get to make such choices and I don't?"

Suddenly, the vase—our mother's vase—burst into a thousand pieces. Lizzie lifted an arm, ducking down, but I was too transfixed by what happened to even think of hiding. A few shards landed on my face, slicing into me, no doubt leaving me with tiny cuts. I winced and brushed them off, but I made no move to call for assistance. I was surprised no one came rushing out to see the cause of the destruction.

"Hannah," Lizzie said, her voice shaky. "You must…your magick is out of control. You must go back and see Thaya. She can help you."

"Stop telling me what to do," I shouted. "Stop treating me like I'm your child. *You* are the one who made mistakes. *You* are the one Father doesn't trust with his own business. What right do you think you have to tell me to do anything?"

Lizzie flinched as if I'd struck her. And perhaps I had. I didn't mean to assault her so callously, even if what I said was true.

"I only want to protect you," she said in a soft voice. "I know what it's like to lose control. I don't want—"

"What?" I threw my arms up. "Tell me, Lizzie. You? Lose control with your—" I stopped myself. I knew people must be listening. I couldn't slip up, not when I would be putting both of us at risk. I only hoped no one witnessed the vase breaking. "I don't believe you."

Lizzie took in a breath. "Why do you think Brendan and I aren't together anymore?" she asked, picking at her fingers. "He discovered I had magick."

I blinked once, twice. "Wait," I said, holding up a hand. "What?"

"He knows, Hannah," she said defensively, crossing her arms over her chest and carefully stepping over the glass.

At that moment, Harold arrived, bedraggled and annoyed. He took the sight of us in, the broken vase, and offered to clean it up. I was sure he wanted to say much more, like, perhaps how we shouldn't be out of bed and we were waking him from his precious slumber. However, he remained silent and seemed grateful when Lizzie shooed him away. We didn't speak until we were certain we were both alone once more.

"He can't even look at me," she said, striding over to the vase and kneeling. "You've seen it. He barely speaks a word to me."

"How does he know?" I made my way next to her to help her. "You've always been careful."

"I have," she agreed. "But surely you know what it's like to be in a position where emotions get the better of you."

I couldn't be sure in the candlelight, but her cheeks seemed to heat up as she carefully picked up the glass.

"I..." I looked back at the mess I made. "Clearly, I'm familiar with what you speak of. I've experienced it myself."

"With Adrian?" Lizzie asked. There didn't seem to be any judgment in her tone. If anything, she was...curious. The tilt of her head, the way her hair fell over her shoulder, left her more vulnerable than I would have expected from her. If anything, it made me want to talk to her about this, even if I didn't fully trust her.

"Y-yes," I admitted. I turned away. I didn't want her to read my face, or myself for that matter. Instead, I focused on picking up the pieces without cutting myself.

"Did he leave?" Lizzie asked. "Is that why the two of you stopped seeing each other?"

"Adrian has never been afraid of what I can do," I said, without thinking about how that might come out. "If anything, he's awed by me."

"Why did you stop seeing him then?" Lizzie asked.

"You easily forget how you treated him." I arched a brow, glancing at her briefly before turning back to clean the glass. "When you discovered him in my room?"

"What do you expect, Han?" she asked. "He runs a brothel. Clearly, he has *experience*. I couldn't let him ruin you, could I? It is my duty as your sister to protect you and your reputation, especially since mine is in shambles. One of us must make Father proud. One of us must bear the burden. And unfortunately, dear sister, it must be you. I don't regret that."

"Well, I do," I snapped. "I regret a lot of what's happened between me and you. I regret you used your magick on me even though we promised ourselves we would never do such a thing. I regret I rejected Adrian's request for help out of turn. I regret my ignorance, my judgment, my trust and my faith in you. I regret all of it."

The wall paintings in the foyer began to shake. I knew it was because of me and my rising temper, but I didn't know how to stop myself. My temper had been activated, and everything I had been holding back, everything I kept quiet about, was coming to the forefront and I couldn't prevent myself from airing it all out.

"I regret going with you to Thaya because I don't trust her," I continued. "And I rue the day I fell into this role of complying daughter, genteel daughter, bound by her duty to her family, so easily." I wrinkled my nose in disgust. "As someone who possesses certain liberties, Lizzie, I would expect you to know what a cage feels like to live in since you've been in my position and somehow freed yourself. I would have expected you, as my sister, to teach me how I can do the same for myself, but instead, you let me rot in here alone since Father's attention was on me rather than you. Since you could do what you wanted because at least Father had me to pay attention to."

Lizzie paled during my speech and hurt flashed across her eyes, but I didn't care. She needed to hear this. More than that, I needed to say it. I needed to get this burden off my chest, as it had become too heavy, suffocating me.

"I want nothing to do with Father's business," I said, throwing my arms out. Paintings started to fall around me. "I want nothing to do with Thaya's training. I want to know who I am and what I'm capable of, and why it's manifesting now. And you could have told me what you discovered about yourself when you began your training with Thaya, but you didn't. You kept it from me. I'm your sister, Lizzie. We're supposed to share everything. We're supposed to trust each other. But you don't trust me! And I...I don't trust you. And I hate I can't rely on you to be someone who can help me, who I can count on."

Suddenly, my head throbbed. I got dizzy and reached for the wall, something to help me steady myself.

"Hannah." Lizzie reached out to help me, but I threw myself backward, nearly falling myself.

"Don't touch me!" I all but screeched. I knew I was causing disruption and the servants would stir. They would come here, and witness our fight. They would gossip about us for the next week if not two.

I had to get out of here. I had to leave before I did something I would regret. I stumbled toward the door, my fingers wrapping around the knobs.

Lizzie's eyes narrowed. "Where are you going?" she demanded to know. "It'll be daybreak soon. You can't be out there alone, Hannah, it's dangerous."

She wasn't wrong. I knew this. But I couldn't help myself. I needed air. I needed to be away from her. I needed...something. I didn't know what that was, but I knew I wouldn't find it here.

I pulled the door open and stumbled outside. The cold morning air was like a slap to my face. It should have brought me to my senses, righted my thoughts so I would be a good little girl and return home, go back inside.

But I couldn't go back in there. Not yet.

I wasn't sure where I was going, but my feet led me away from the house, through the gates. I wasn't sure where the guards were, though perhaps they didn't recognize me because no one stopped me.

I thought Lizzie would come after me. She was much more athletic than I was, and she'd be able to catch me with ease.

But she never did.

Perhaps I should have been disappointed she let me leave so easily, but I started to laugh with relief. I was free. Maybe not forever. But I was free. My feet led me to the brothel, which wasn't all that surprising. Just as I was about to let myself in, Adrian came out. His eyes widened at the sight of me before sweeping up and down my body, like he expected me to be injured.

"Are you well?" he asked gruffly.

"Yes," I said and couldn't stop a smile from forming.

He tilted his head to the side, clearly confused. "Then why are you here?" he asked. "Won't you be missing?"

"Take me to your ship," I said. My hands shook, my heart beat hard inside my chest, but I met his eyes without flinching. "Please. I don't want to be alone right now."

CHAPTER FIFTEEN

Hannah

I shouldn't have been surprised Adrian listened to me. He wasn't the type to tell me I should go home. And I knew I shouldn't be alone with him.

But he obeyed me without question, and even now, as I stood on the deck of his ship, as my skin prickled with goosebumps from the cold—or so I told myself—I was relieved. He had carried me to his ship. Because of his speed, it wasn't far. I had been here before. I tipped my chin up, just as I always did when I wanted to feign confidence I wasn't feeling now.

I looked toward the ship's stern, a silhouette against the lightening sky. It resembled a masterpiece hanging in one of the manor's hallways, and not a picture of my current reality. The faint moon was first quarter, as if someone had covered it with an inky piece of parchment, drawing a line down the center. Faded stars still shone, sprinkling the sky like a million dying fireflies.

A throat cleared behind me and I turned to meet Adrian's gaze. I saw the hunger in his eyes, and my heart thumped in my chest like a rabbit fleeing a fox. He seemed to read something in my return stare as he swiftly crossed the small space between us until he was towering over me.

I didn't back away. Not this time.

Everything screamed at me to run, to leave, even if it meant throwing myself off his ship to save myself from him. But tonight, I didn't want to be saved.

Adrian tilted his head down, watching me as if expecting me to pull away and run. When I didn't, when his lips found my neck and I sighed, his eyes widened, and that was his moment of realization I wanted this.

He consumed me. His lips drew patterns on my skin, his tongue writing a secret language I didn't understand. My knees buckled and I would have crumpled to the floor of the ship if it hadn't been for his arms coiling around my waist, squeezing me tightly to his body like a snake. I buried my fingers in his tunic, wrinkling the silk. Basking in the sensual sensation of it between each digit, a soft reminder this moment was occurring; this wasn't a dream.

I gasped when he found a particularly sensitive spot, where my neck and shoulder met. He lingered there for a moment before gently sucking at the skin, and I knew it could leave a mark there in the morning.

I knew what this man was, what he could do to me, and my grip on him tightened, torn between pulling away and running or staying exactly where I was. I chose to cling to him tighter. His hand still held my cheek, fingers splayed across my skin, keeping my face exactly where he wanted it to be.

"Don't tempt me, darling," he murmured against my skin. His lips vibrated softly, tickling me, overwhelming me so my pelvis throbbed with desire. "Do not offer yourself to me only to pull it away under the guise of your highborn charm."

"I…" Was that what I was doing? I opened my eyes to look Adrian in the eye. I didn't want him to stop and I didn't want him to think I was simply using him because I'd had a long day.

"Perhaps we should rest," he said. He started to pull away from me but I wouldn't let him go.

"No," I said, more firmly than I expected to. He raised his brows, surprised by my challenge, but I held my ground. "No. I'm not…that isn't…"

"I will not be used as a game, Hannah," he said, each word clipped. The sudden anger that seemed to consume him made me flinch, but I didn't back away. "What happened? Did you fight with your father and, in some act of rebellion, you've come to me to take away your purity? I will not do it."

"I... That's not why..." My voice trailed off, unsure. Maybe he was right. Lizzie and I had fought because I didn't like the girl she saw me as. Maybe throwing myself at Adrian was my ploy to get her to see me as something more.

"Don't lie to me," he said. "Because once I allow myself the privilege of claiming you, you will be mine. I can't just let you go. This isn't a game. This is fire. And you'd better prepare yourself to get burned should you decide to play with it."

"I'm not lying to you," I said. "I came here because I realized every part of my life has been controlled by everyone else. Even Thaya doesn't think I can learn magick on my own. And yet, I feel like I'm on the wrong path." I tried to search for the words, tried to figure out just how I wanted to tell Adrian how I felt, but I couldn't quite articulate it. "I just know I want to be with you. I'm not...I'm not expecting marriage or even love from you. I know what you are. I know you'll break my heart. But I want to be with you regardless."

"Why?" he asked, searching my eyes for the answer. "Why would you want that, knowing it'll never be what you want?"

"I don't know," I admitted. "I only know when I think about it, it's always you. And I feel like I'm actually in control and out of control at the same time, which doesn't make much sense to me, but it's my feeling no one can control. And I want to hang on to it, on to you, for as long as I can."

"You told me we were to part ways after discovering the truth of the missing Sirens," he pointed out.

I wasn't sure what to say to that. He wasn't wrong. Yet the thought of me not seeing him again felt like someone reaching into my chest and forcing me to live without my heart. At the same time, I didn't want to continue to barter with him. "If you don't wish for my presence, I can leave. I'm sure there's someone else I can go to, someone else willing to have me."

I didn't mean the words. They were lies, and I was positive Adrian knew I was lying, knew I would never leave to seek out someone else, even for company.

But still, he growled at the thought of me with someone else, extending his fangs and stalking toward me. Whenever I was around him, I felt like prey, but it wasn't until now, seeing his shoulders hunched, ready to lunge for me, that I truly believed it. The wind tousled my hair, the gentle movement of his ship swaying back and forth soothing. I was sure he could feel the vibrations of my rapidly beating heart.

"You belong to me, Hannah Walker," he growled, and tiny lightning bolts shot straight to my pelvis. My body throbbed with desire.

Suddenly, a break in the sky interrupted the moment. The sun was on its way up. I wasn't sure of the lore of Blood Mages, but I believed as long as Adrian was on his ship, it didn't matter if the sun touched his skin. Which meant we could stay here if we wanted to.

Until rain began to fall, hard and unforgiving. The hard tapping of the water hitting the wood was a symphony. My dress clung to my body, my hair tangled in damp knots on my face and the back of my neck. It was a cold rain, one that elicited goosebumps and chills down spines.

Adrian scooped me up and took me in his arms until we were in his cabin. His body was abnormally cooler than a human's and yet still I felt his heat.

"You fear me," he said, slowly peeling himself away from me. He chose to stand behind his desk, putting distance between us. Whether it was for my protection or his, I didn't know.

"No," I said immediately. "I'm…I'm nervous. I've never done…" I let my voice trail off. I didn't have to go into details about my lack of experience. Surely he knew I had never done this before.

Adrian's eyes grew darker, contrasting with a peek of light seeping through the dark storm.

"I'm well aware of your innocence," he murmured roughly. His fingers grasped the edge of the desk and I was sure he was going to break off a piece of the wood with his vise-like grip.

"Why do you think you entice me so much?" He clenched his teeth together. "Too much."

A little prickle of power shot through me. I was confronted with the possibility this was as difficult for him as it was for me, that our situations were more alike than I'd initially assumed. I was certain Adrian's experience made him some sort of predator, taking advantage of my ignorance. But perhaps, he was as drawn to me and my purity as the way that moth he liked to talk about was drawn to a flame.

Power wasn't something I was used to feeling. But I didn't want to release that feeling any time soon. I wanted to hold on to it for as long as I could. I never got to experience it, and now…maybe that would change.

"You want me," I said.

He tilted his head to the side. "Haven't I told you as much?" He leaned forward, his corded muscles rippling through the tunic he wore. "Don't you believe me when I tell you you're are mine? When I showed up at your house, when I marked your neck, when I—"

I placed a finger on his lips to keep him from talking any longer. He was getting frustrated, but I wasn't afraid of him. I hadn't even realized I crossed the room to his desk until I shushed him with my finger to his mouth. His eyes widened in awe and he blinked, almost confused at my forward action.

"I have dreams," I said slowly. "When I'm alone in my bed. When I close my eyes, you're there, touching me in places I haven't touched myself." It was difficult to even admit such things to myself, let alone him, but it was time. The words spilt out of me like petals falling from a flower. "And I crave it. I crave you. And my fear builds because I want you so much, even if I think this could be the biggest mistake of my entire life. I know what I want. I've been denying myself ever since you forced your way into my life. And

I'm tired of doing it. I don't…I don't wish to run from you, Adrian. Not any longer."

His throat bobbed as he took in my words. I could only hope it meant he was listening, that he took what I had to say seriously. I sucked in a breath, released it, and then held it.

He had yet to respond. Nothing was telling on his chiseled face, save for the way his icy blue eyes turned dark, like the sky late at night. I wanted to fall into those eyes, drown myself in them, only as long as he continued to look at me the way he was looking at me now.

"Foolish mortal," he breathed out. "You offer yourself to me like a sacrifice. That isn't what I want from you."

I frowned slightly, trying to understand what I did wrong, where I miscalculated—until he leaned in. His cheek pressed against mine and he inhaled deeply like he wanted to capture my very essence.

"What *do* you want from me?" I whispered. I held my breath, almost afraid of what he would say, what he would ask of me.

He pulled back so he could look into my eyes.

"When I claim you, it won't be because I want you for your innocence," he said. "I want you because it's you. Because you've wormed your way inside of me and left me haunted by your ghost. I want to taste you, to feel you, to fuck you, to hear you say my name in the throes of passion and know you know you belong to me and only me. I want your very essence, your very soul. I want you to bring me to life in a way no one ever has before, Hannah. I am not alive, and I am not dead. I am in stasis, in between two worlds. I want you to be my bridge. I want your anger and fear, your joy and pleasure. I want to sink my fangs into your flesh and feed from you, the very catalyst to send you into wave after wave of pleasure. I want you writhing, screaming, fighting. I want…I want *you*."

He was breathless by the end of it. As was I. And I reveled in it.

"Then take me," I said. "I'm yours."

CHAPTER SIXTEEN

Hannah

I held my breath and waited.

I wasn't quite sure what I expected him to do. I thought he might lunge for me the way he had when he kissed me. He might pin me to the wall behind me and assault my throat with kisses. He might rip off my clothes and explore my body with his hands, fill me up and make me his in a way no one ever had before.

Instead, Adrian merely stared at me, almost as though he expected this to turn out to be some sort of jest.

"Do not toy with me, Hannah," he finally said. "I will not ruin you for sport."

"I'm not asking you to ruin me," I said. The word wasn't right, not for what I had in mind. For what I hoped would happen between us. "I want you to make do on your promises, Adrian. I want you to please me. I want to learn about myself in ways I never could have imagined. I want to be yours, just like you said." Suddenly, I jerked back. "I do not ask for any commitment if that's what you're worried about. I just...I want you to give me freedom in a way I can't even fathom. Please."

Adrian stared again, his intense gaze sending chills down my spine. I wasn't sure if the shudder was because I was afraid or unsure. However, I knew what I wanted.

"I'm asking you to ravish me—"

"There will be no ravishing," he insisted. "You aren't ready."

I jerked my head back, affronted. "I am," I insisted, stomping over there. "Adrian, I—"

"Your inexperience has your body tight," he said. "I can feel it, Hannah. You aren't ready for a ravishing. You must first get used to the sensation. I warn you, it can be painful."

"Why must you insist on treating me like a child who does not know her mind?" I asked.

He stared back at me, eyes serious. "It isn't my intention to treat you that way, Hannah," he said, his voice surprisingly gentle. "I only want you to be certain of what you want. Because there is no going back after this. Your emotions are getting the better of you—"

"My emotions are showing me exactly what I want," I said, interrupting him. "And that's you. Please, Adrian."

"Are you going to threaten to find someone else if I say no?" he all but growled.

I sighed and looked away. "No," I admitted, feeling a little annoyed. I didn't want to have to beg. "Adrian, if you prefer women with more experience than I—"

"Don't be a fool," he snapped. "You are all I want."

He leaned his forehead against mine. My heart fluttered. He was going to kiss me again. I was sure of it. This was exactly what I wanted.

When he took a step back, placed his hands on my hips, and turned me around to face the wall, I wasn't sure what he meant to do. I tried to look at him over my shoulder, but he deftly turned my face forward and placed my hands flat against the wall.

"Time to feel, not see," he said silkily, the words sending a thrill to my groin. His fingers deftly untied the lace to my corset. I shivered in delight at the touch of his fingers on my naked skin.

"Your heart beats like that of a caught canary," he whispered. His breath warmed the slope of my neck, causing goosebumps to run down the length of my spine.

"You can hear it?" He'd already mentioned being able to hear my heart, but it still awed me.

"I can hear everything," he said teasingly. He finally had my corset loose and slid his hands under the material to let it fall to the ground. Cool air caressed my bare skin, and I sucked in a breath that had nothing to do with it. Instead, Adrian's hands remained on my bare waist, fingers tracing patterns into my skin. My head leaned back as I let myself feel Adrian touch me without anything inhibiting him from doing so. I rested on his broad shoulder and closed my eyes, taking in another heavy breath.

"You're warm," he murmured. His lips ghosted over my throat, lingering like he was marking his target, like he knew exactly what part of me he wanted to focus on first.

"Yes," I managed to say. I wasn't sure what else I could say and I felt compelled to respond to him. My nipples marbled under the exposure to the air, goosebumps erupting all over my body. I was exposed and it felt so good.

I felt a gentle pressure on my hips, forcing me to turn around. I obeyed. I stood before him like an erotic painting, exposed to his hungry gaze. He took me in, feasting on me without shame.

There was something surprisingly empowering about the attention Adrian fixed on me, the way his eyes darkened to a midnight blue, the way his jaw locked in place. The instinct to cover myself up was overwhelming, but I overrode it.

I wanted him to see me, to see who I was underneath it all.

Adrian wrapped his hands around my hips, pulling me closer to him. For the first time in my life, I felt a man's hardness against me and it made me blush with both heat and embarrassment.

He was now lavishing his attention on my neck with his mouth. My skin was pinched between his lips, and I knew I was going to bruise. I simply didn't care.

He led me to his bed, which was placed in the center of the room, one side against the wall. Red silk sheets wrapped around the mattress. The second the back of my knees hit it, I leaned back, flinching at the cold and attempting to warm myself up while keeping my focus on Adrian and what he was doing to my body.

His hands trailed down the curves of my body in light caresses. It was everything I wanted, everything I craved. I had never been touched this way before, and I found wanted more of it.

"You are perfect," he murmured, picking his head up so he could lock eyes with me. "Everything about you is perfect."

It was a hard thing for me to believe about myself because I knew exactly what all of my flaws were. But I could hear the reverence in his tone so I accepted his words of the promise he found me alluring.

His mouth trailed down my chest until his lips found my left breast and he tugged at my nipple. My eyes snapped open and I gasped at the incredibly sensual sensation, my groin flooding with heat and need. I reached for Adrian and dug my fingers into his hair, tugging at the roots. He sucked at my tender breast like an animal, and the thought he was feeding his basic needs caused my pelvis to throb with desire.

Adrian captured my gaze with his own, his hands keeping me in place. My heart began to stutter and I threw my head back and embraced the sensations writhing through my body.

His left hand crept up and massaged my other breast, causing my nipples to throb under his gentle caress.

I needed this, needed more.

My grip on him tightened and I let out a moan. The sound filled the silence as Adrian moved his mouth to my other breast, his right hand now on the one he'd released. He explored it with the same fervor he had with the first one, the lavish attention causing tiny little sparks to come together and set my body on fire.

He pressed into me. I could feel his hardness against my hipbone, and my heart skipped a beat at the feel of it against me. There was something both alluring and intimidating about the feel of him. He pulled away, and I slid my fingers under his tunic, pulling the sides apart so it fell open and revealed his bare chest. He was glorious, with muscles packed against his torso like some kind of shield, protecting him. Before I could stop myself, I ran my hands up and down his torso. I needed to feel his muscles as they twitched under my touch, see if he was as hard as he looked.

He gently pushed open my thighs. The cool air caressed my lower body, and I knew I wanted more of his touch. When his finger pressed against my mound, I let out a garbled moan, arching my back to seek his touch out even more.

"Gods, you're dripping," Adrian murmured, more to himself than to me. I whimpered as he continued to touch me. I didn't know how to put into words what I wanted but I knew I didn't want him to stop.

"Hannah."

His strained voice forced me to look up at him. His eyes still feasted on my naked body. "You must...tell me. Tell me to stop. Please, tell me to stop before I succumb."

"I don't want you to stop," I said.

"It will hurt," he warned.

"Yes."

"You will bleed."

"Yes."

He swallowed, almost as though he was surprised I'd still be willing to trust him with this despite what it might mean for me.

"I'm not afraid," I told him. "Not with you."

This seemed to be exactly what he needed to hear. He claimed my mouth as he positioned himself over me. Without breaking the kiss, he pushed into my folds slowly. His cock was thick and stretched me farther than I expected. I sunk my nails into his back, clinging to him for dear life. He wasn't even inside me all the way and tears already blurred my vision. I held my breath. Waited. I loosened my grip slightly.

The smell of something subtly musky filled the air. Adrian clenched his teeth together, eyes darkening even further. "You're mine, Hannah. You're mine. You'll always be mine." He kissed my face, my neck. "Gods, you're slick with desire."

"It's all for you," I managed to get out. He stilled at my words, and we locked eyes once again. Finally, after what felt like an extended amount of time, my body grew accustomed to his size. I tilted my hips up, rolling them slightly, feeling bolder, and I groaned at the waves of pleasure flooding my body. Adrian didn't need to be encouraged again. He began to rock back and forth inside of me, slowly at first, until we were both panting and clinging to each other. Adrian traced my throat with his tongue before taking the sensitive flesh between his lips and pressing down. My pelvis twitched uncontrollably. Stars sparkled over my vision as I fell into nothing, into everything. Adrian was the only thing that grounded me in this reality. Pleasure washed through me like wave after wave, and by the time it eased downward, I was breathless. My entire body tingled with satiated sensitivity and warmth flooded my chest. Adrian let out a long groan as he released himself inside of me, not stopping until we were both spent, shaking with pleasure even after Adrian pulled away. His arms wrapped possessively around my waist, he buried his face in my tangled hair, and, with our legs still entwined, we slept.

CHAPTER SEVENTEEN

Adrian

I wanted more of her.

This was the worst thing that could have possibly happened to me. I'd been certain possessing Hannah in this way would rid my craving for her. She'd no longer haunt me.

But now, I wanted her even more.

I looked at her lying peacefully in the shadows of my bed. Her porcelain perfection drew me to her like a moth to a flame, a bumblebee to a beautiful flower. I reached out and swept my fingers down her throat. Her head was tilted to the side, eyes closed in slumber, giving me better access to it.

The sudden urge to bury my fangs inside of her, to penetrate her in that way, to feast off her, to draw her inside of me so I could never rid myself of her, overwhelmed me. Now I understood how it felt to be inside of her, to be smothered with her purity, with her gentle, innocent affection for a monster like me.

I was addicted, and I'd only been with her once.

The animal inside me urged me to kill her. It told me to wrap my fingers around her throat and squeeze the life from her body, so she could never realize how much power she held over me. Because she *would* one day wield it to her advantage. She would use it, use me, like I was nothing more than clay being molded into something else, someone I wasn't. I knew I would do anything she asked me to, and I hated her for it.

Maybe the animal was right. My succumbing to these feelings had clawed their way inside of me and held me hostage to my rational thought.

But—I knew I could no more harm her than I could myself.

She blinked open her eyes once, twice, and stifled a yawn. Hannah was so deliriously…human. And she was mine. She was mine, and I could no longer deny it.

I leaned forward and claimed her lips. What was supposed to be a passionate proclamation of ownership and possession became softer, almost tender. She tasted so sweet, and I couldn't resist. Her eyes, forest green and captivating as a sunrise, pulled me into their depths, and it was then I realized how completely ensnared I was. She may be mine. But I belonged to her too. She owned me and that was my undoing.

My body stirred simply because of her kisses, of her touching me, and I leaned over her and positioned myself on top of her again. She continued to hold my stare, seemingly unafraid but still nervous. Her trusting gaze humbled me. No one had ever looked at me the way Hannah Walker was looking at me right now. I hated how badly the urge of wanting to be worthy of such a look rose in me.

She wrapped her slim legs around my waist, and I eased myself into her, knowing she was probably still tender and raw from before. Her body consumed mine and if she was feeling the effects of her first time, it didn't show. She was slick with her desire for me, taking all of me in, inch by inch.

Her entire face was overwhelmed by pleasure, the pleasure I was giving her. Pride swelled in my chest. Ensuring my lovers received their pleasure was of great importance to me, but there was something different about it being Hannah, that eradicated all the rest of my lovers until they were nothing but dust, grains of sand on a meaningless shore.

Hannah was my ocean, consuming me, breathing life into me. She sighed when I was fully enveloped by her warmth.

I pushed her wild hair from her neck so I could access her throat. Even now, I could see the marks on her pale skin, indicating she was mine, mine, mine. I traced them each with a finger, counting four little bruises I wanted to make bigger, wanted to show everyone.

God, she was beautiful. She was everything I thought I'd never have.

My hands traced the curves of her body as if I could mold her into my very definition of perfection. But the truth was, I wouldn't change a thing about her. She was perfection defined as if she'd been created solely to give me everything I wanted.

I knew how arrogant that was, but I didn't care. I knew she could choose to be with a different man, a human, someone who would fall to their feet at the prospect of bedding her.

My thrusts became harder, more demanding, at the thought of her with anyone else. I couldn't stomach the idea another man would claim her in this way. My fingers wrapped around her shoulder, her waist, digging into the silky flesh. I needed her to understand she was mine without saying the words, without telling her the truth, because this was so much more than simple possession. I didn't just want her body or her innocence. I wanted her mind. I wanted her smart tongue and to worship the freckles on her face. I wanted the very essence of who she was, and I wanted to brand it with my name so everyone knew who she belonged to.

I groaned, buried so deeply inside of Hannah, at the thought happiness was possible for me.

I stopped moving for a moment, just to look down, to see her expression. Her green eyes burned with desire, bruised mouth dropped open into a silent gasp. But there was more than just the pleasure she was receiving from me. I could read her emotions so easily and could feel the warmth not only from her slick, soft folds but from her very heart.

She would give me anything I asked for. Perhaps she'd even let me feed on her.

I looked away. I knew she couldn't read my thoughts, but I still didn't want her to have any sort of clue as to what I was thinking about.

"Adrian," she said huskily. "Are you all right?"

I didn't respond. Instead, I thrust deeper into her, deeper than I thought was possible. Her face contorted into both pain and pleasure, and when I did it again, she clutched my shoulders, letting out a soft moan.

Her sounds were my undoing. They put me in some sort of trance. I increased my pace, She made me…animalistic. Made me lose my senses, my control.

This slip of a human had me bound to her in every way imaginable, and I had no qualms about such a bond. I wanted it, let her have her advantage over me. I would help her dig my grave and bury me herself. Hannah met each thrust with her hips, taking me in all the way, helping propel me even deeper. She didn't seem to mind this wasn't love, this act between us, but dominance. Pure possession. And yet, she gave as good as she got. Her eyes sparkled with want, with need, and I realized she wanted this too. She wanted to be claimed by me.

"Adrian," she managed to get out. My name from her mouth was like an enchantment, a spell she cast over me. I would do anything for her when she said my name that way. "Adrian, please."

"Please, what?" I managed to get out. "Tell me, Hannah. Tell me what you want for me and I will do it. I will do anything."

Her eyes closed and her mouth fell open. She seemed lost in the buildup of pleasure so speech was lost. Pride flared in my chest. Bestowing pleasure to her was what she wanted and I could give it to her.

I would give her anything she asked me, anything at all. "Don't," she finally got out, opening her eyes and locking them with mine. "Don't stop. Please don't stop."

I almost spilt everything I had in her right then. I refused to empty myself so quickly, especially when she had yet to experience her pleasure. I couldn't embarrass myself in such a way.

I could feel the strain in her body, the way it yearned to find its release. She tilted her head to the side, revealing the marks on her neck to me once again, and I was lost.

I needed her to come, to take me with her, because I was floating out here by myself, and I didn't want to be alone any longer. Not when she looked like she did.

Her mouth dropped open and her eyes fluttered closed as she orgasmed, and suddenly, I was swimming in an ocean with no depth, an ocean that filled the sky. I didn't stop, couldn't stop until she'd drained every last drop from me. Only then did I collapse next to her. I pulled her into my arms, burying myself in her hair, lips grazing her shoulder, needing her warmth, needing the reassurance this was something real I could hold on to.

Hannah's eyes were still closed as she relaxed against me. Her fingers dragged along my skin, and I realized then, basking in this afterglow of our intimacy, that I was hers just as much as she was mine. Instead of running from it, I had to lean in. I had to admit the truth of this before she slipped away.

"I can't let you go," I murmured, my voice raw.

"Hmm. Then don't," she murmured sleepily.

"There are bruises on your neck," I said. "Where I bit you."

She opened her eyes but didn't speak. It seemed as though she was waiting for me to explain something.

"You can't return home with those marks on your neck," I said, pushing hair from her face.

"Oh." She blushed. "I haven't thought about returning home, but you're right. I should—"

"You're welcome here for as long as you need, Hannah," I told her. "But I don't wish to keep you from your family. My only concern is your reputation." I brushed my knuckles on her throat and smirked when she closed her eyes and shuddered. "I can get rid of them, though."

"How?" She slowly opened her eyes, pinning me in place.

"Take my blood," I explained. "A drop. Two."

She looked at my mouth but didn't immediately reject the idea.

"I must warn you, though, because I fed recently on you, this would symbolize an exchange of blood," I continued. Because she needed to know. I wouldn't trick her.

"Okay," she said. "What does that mean?"

"It means we would be bonded," I said. "And that would be a deeper thing than your human form of matrimony. Is it something you'd want…with me?"

CHAPTER EIGHTEEN

Hannah

The thought of taking Adrian's blood caused my loins to ache. I didn't understand how such a thing was possible, considering Adrian and I had just made love twice. I didn't expect my body to be able to handle any more of him, any more of the pleasure wrought on me with his wicked mouth and his hard body. And yet, my body still craved him in every way. I was insatiable for his attention and wanted nothing more than to mount him like a horse and ride him until I derived my pleasure from him.

Instead, I began to play with the ends of my hair, needing something to distract myself with before I succumbed fully to my desires. He was asking a good question, and he deserved the respect from me to answer.

"I'm not sure," I said slowly. "I know we've been intimate. Twice. But that doesn't seem to be cause for such a union between the two of us." I thought Adrian would have been offended. Instead, the corners of his lips twitched up and his blue eyes sparkled with mischief, something I hadn't expected to see from him.

"My, my, Hannah," he said in a gentle, teasing voice. "You cause scandal wherever you go, don't you? Here I am, offering you marriage, and you reject me because you don't think we've been intimate enough." Without warning, he rolled on top of me, pinning me into place. My heart leapt in my throat out of both anticipation and fear. "How many times must I have my wicked way with you before you'll agree?"

I started to laugh, despite myself. "Come, now, Adrian," I said. "Certainly, you don't wish to bond yourself to me so quickly, if at all."

He propped his elbow onto the bed, resting his cheek in his palm. "And what makes you say that?" he asked. His hand found my hip and he began to rub my skin with his fingers, tracing mindless patterns into my skin. It was almost as though he was gently branding me, insisting I belonged to him even in the simplest of gestures.

"Marriage, Adrian?" I asked, shifting so I was lying on my back. It was important to me to look at him, to gauge whether he was making a mockery of institutionalized marriage or if he meant what he said. "I'd expect from you, that's a bit much."

"That's an assumption," he said.

"Have you ever been in love before?" I asked. When he remained silent, I pressed on. "You haven't. You admitted as much to me. And here you are, asking to form some kind of bond with me that's stronger than marriage." I let out a breath. "I don't understand why." I narrowed my eyes slightly. "I will not be made a fool."

"You are my little fool," he said lightly, ghosting a kiss on my neck.

"Don't tease me," I insisted, ignoring the way goosebumps consumed my flesh. "I'm not trying to trap you into a marriage or a bond or anything you might feel like you can't get out of. I only ask you don't mock my feelings."

"I'm doing no such thing, and the fact you keep insisting I am is starting to get trying." He pulled away from me, only to give me a long look. "I would never offer you something I didn't want to give you. You must take what I say seriously or you show me you trust me with your body and not your heart."

"I didn't think you even wanted my heart," I said. My voice came out harsher than I intended, and I dropped my gaze to my chest, covered with the silk sheets Adrian had on his bed. I wrapped them tighter around my body because I could feel a chill start to claw its way in the air.

"I want all of you," he insisted. "I have said as much. Why don't you believe me?"

"Because I'm not certain I'm the first woman you've ever said such a thing to," I said. I tilted my head to the side and looked into his eyes. "I am not naive, Adrian. I know men make promises they have no intention of keeping. They say exactly what you want to hear until you discover them in a lie. And then they've ruined you, they've shredded any semblance of faith you might have had in them, which is tragic because you're the only one who believed in them in the first place."

Adrian reached out and gently pushed a curl from my hair. "It sounds, darling, as though you speak of someone specific," he said. "Would you care to indulge me as to who it could be?"

I sighed. I didn't wish to speak of this at all, much less to Adrian. It was still a place of contention for me, a bruise I had ignored but still ached when I poked it.

"Not particularly," I said, avoiding eye contact. Adrian stared at me as if willing me to look at him. I held out for as long as I could. The last thing I wanted was for him to push me into spilling my heart. And yet, the fact he wasn't demanding answers as he rubbed his fingers up and down my arm patiently, causing my guts to tug, I knew, at that moment, I'd give him anything he asked of me.

I already had. I sighed dejectedly, shifting until I was on my side and could meet his eyes. "Henry Davenport, the Lead of Ankura's Patrol," I clarified when I saw Adrian knit his brow together.

"The one who reeked of alcohol and jealousy when we looked at Claire Turner's body that night," he stated.

I nodded. "Yes," I said. "The two of us were romantically involved two years ago when I was fifteen. I was certain he was going to propose." I reached out and clasped Adrian's upper arm. I needed something to hold on to, something to soothe and stabilize me. "I was deliriously in love with him. He was handsome and witty and when he looked at me, I didn't have to wonder if he felt the same. I knew it to be true."

"You speak as though you harbor feelings for him still," he pointed out. There was an edge to his voice, but it wasn't as harsh as I expected it to be.

"I don't," I said. My voice wasn't insisting; I had nothing to prove. If Adrian didn't believe my assertion, that was his choice. "Once I discovered his love of drink as his only method to cope with trials and tribulations, I threw myself into helping him overcome it. I learned there was no point in doing such a thing if he didn't want to overcome anything. He had to want to be better. Instead, he wanted nothing of the sort. He didn't think his addiction was a problem and reveled in it even though he knew I was never comfortable around him when he drank excessively."

"Would he become violent with you, Hannah?" Adrian asked dangerously. I didn't like the way it sounded; like he would punish Henry depending on the next thing I said. It was a shot fired, a warning.

"Never," I told him truthfully. "But there was one time we were out and about town, just the two of us. It was a beautiful day. The weather was gorgeous. The sun shone down, sparkling the sea. The breeze ruffled my skirt but didn't leave a chill. It was something." My lips curved just thinking about it. "We were celebrating. Henry had been with Patrol for months, and he'd received his first promotion. He found me immediately after learning of the news. He insisted we celebrate. I was all too happy to do so. I thought, with every fiber of my being, this would inspire him to be a better man if I couldn't. And while it hurt knowing I wasn't worth the sacrifice, I wanted him to change regardless. If I didn't inspire it and his new job did, I would take that as a victory."

Adrian's fingers began tracing the curves of my body, and I sighed in contentment. Something was soothing about his touch. Strange, knowing he could kill me with those same fingers gently exploring my body.

"And?" he urged, his voice low.

"I thought it was my presence he wanted when he meant he wanted to celebrate," I said, closing my eyes so I could feel Adrian, but didn't have to see his face. "And, to a degree, it was. But he merely wanted company at his favorite tavern. And as selfish as it was, I refused. I wouldn't spend a beautiful day in some dimly lit tavern that smelled of feces and piss and spilt alcohol. I wouldn't endure strange men undressing me with their eyes or touching me and claiming they tripped. I'd already done that before. When I addressed my concerns with Henry, he waved them off, telling me I was being irrational. We fought. He told me I ruined his day, his promotion. He said vile things, and I'm not happy to admit I said some things in return. It was only then I realized I didn't want this for my life. So, I left."

"Did he let you go so easily?"

I scrunched my brow and turned to look at him. "What do you mean?" I asked.

"Well, if I were him, I wouldn't be okay with you simply leaving, even if it was because of a flaw I needed to correct," Adrian said.

"You're saying you would change something to ensure I didn't leave you?" I asked, not bothering to hide my disbelief.

"In truth, I'm not sure," he admitted. "Though I doubt you're the type to demand compliance."

I widened my eyes before I slowly dropped my gaze to the sheets beginning to fall from my chest. I snuggled deeper underneath them, trying to obtain more warmth for myself.

"I didn't," I said. "I told him I didn't like the man he turned into when he drank because he was cruel and cold. But I was desperately in love with him when he was sober. I just couldn't keep doing it. I didn't like how I felt or who I was when I was around him. It was the hardest thing I had to do, breaking ties with him. I cried in my room for a week. Lizzie forced me to get out of bed after a while, and took me to visit my cousins, where they distracted me with plays and good food." I chuckled at the memory.

"How did he take the rejection?" Adrian asked.

I sighed. "Well, you've seen our interactions," I said. "He isn't happy."

"He's still in love with you," he pointed out.

I scoffed. "He hates me," I corrected.

"Perhaps. But I find love and hate are a reflection of the same passion. He would take you back in a heartbeat should you ever change your mind and return to him."

"I have no intention of changing my mind," I said slowly. "Even if he were to change, even if he wanted to be the man I knew he could be, I still wouldn't resume our relationship. It shouldn't have taken me leaving for him to take me seriously. He should have wanted to better himself before I chose to do something this drastic." I glanced over at him, chewing my bottom lip. "I suppose that's why I hesitate to give you my blood."

"Why?"

"I want to," I told him. "I remember what it was like to take your blood. How much pleasure I derived from it. But I'm worried it won't be good enough for you, that you won't like it. I can't bond myself to you unless I'm certain you want me for life, Adrian. And your life extends much longer than my own. I couldn't expect you to commit to me in that manner. You run a brothel, for crying out loud. I wouldn't be able to bear it if you broke my heart. If you left me for another."

"You think I would do something like that?" he asked. "Tell me, do you think I let *anyone* feed from me? I admit I partake in feeding on willing humans simply because feeding on farm animals isn't the same and it leaves me wanting more. But I've never allowed anyone to feed on me, or bonded with anyone else."

"Then why me?" I crossed my arms over my chest, bunching the covers up to ensure I was covered and he couldn't be distracted. "Why would you choose me? We don't know each other very well—"

"Arranged marriages ensure the couple knows each other less than we do," he said. "I just know feeding from you will heal your wounds and it will please me."

"And what if…what if it doesn't?" I asked.

Adrian brushed a kiss against the top of my head. I closed my eyes to enjoy the feeling of gentleness, something I hadn't expected from him. He could inspire a multitude of emotions in me, including trust and pleasure, but tenderness wasn't something I expected. I hoped he did it more often.

"I will never force you to do something you don't wish to do, Hannah," he said. He placed another kiss on me, this time on my temple. "I won't persuade you if you are unsure. If you have questions, I will answer them. But you will never have to feel the burden of pressure from me. Do you understand?"

"Why?" I asked. My eyelids were getting heavy. I turned toward Adrian, needing to press my body against his to soothe the tension that had crept up and stayed.

"Why what?" Adrian asked.

"Why will you accept my answer as it is?" I asked. Even Lizzie attempted to change my mind if I did something she didn't agree with.

"Because I respect you," he said simply. Another kiss, this one on my cheek. "And eventually, you will want me, Hannah. Mark my words. You will want me to feast on you. Not out of necessity but because you want to know what it's like. And I will give it to you because I will give you whatever you desire."

My heart skipped a beat at the unspoken promise and I wrapped my arms around him. I wanted to stay awake, to continue to talk, but I couldn't stop the lure of exhaustion. Especially when Adrian held me close to him, and I'd never felt safer than I did right now.

CHAPTER NINETEEN

Hannah

I didn't feel different.

After Adrian helped me dress, I paused to look at my reflection in the mirror, carefully assessing myself. I didn't *look* different. No one could gaze upon me and know what had occurred between Adrian and me. A part of me wished they could, wanted nothing more than for the world to know everything we did so I didn't have to keep this secret.

But Adrian meant more to me than my comfort. I would keep him for as long as he wanted me. I knew, whatever this was, wasn't over even as the two of us prepared to leave his ship.

I stayed much longer than I should have, certain even my father detected my absence, and, when I returned home, I would be in grave trouble. There might even be a chance Father deemed my absence as too scandalous to risk his business. He might have to strip me from such an inheritance.

My heart skipped a beat at the thought. Was it wrong I found myself hoping for such an outcome?

"What is going on in that mind of yours, darling?" Adrian asked as he stepped behind me to slowly lace up my corset. "I heard your heart jump."

"I just…" I glanced at him over my shoulder. "If my father realizes I'm gone and draws conclusions as to why that might be, there's a chance he won't allow me to inherit his business."

Adrian paused, stopping his ministrations as he looked into my eyes over my shoulder through the mirror. "And?" he finally asked.

I fidgeted, despite my best efforts not to. "And I would look forward to such a release."

Adrian said nothing for a long moment. "What do you want out of your life, Hannah?" he finally asked. "Where do you see yourself in a year?"

It was an intimate but fair question. I sighed, trying to think of a response to it. "Well," I said, twisting my fingers. "Before Claire was murdered, I probably would have told you I expected to be engaged to a man my father deemed worthy of me. Perhaps already married. I would still be learning his business. Perhaps I'd be with child—"

Adrian growled, fangs popping out of his mouth like a snap of fingers. My eyebrows rose and I looked at him, waiting.

"You asked," I pointed out. "So I am telling the truth."

"It doesn't mean I have to like what you say," he snapped. "Tell me, would you like it if I told you I expected to be buried cock-deep in one of the whores in my brothel, legs wrapped around my waist, drawing me even deeper, trying to coax a release from me?"

I whipped out my hand, ready to slap him. He caught my wrist before I could. A light tug at the corners of his lips indicated a smirk was about to appear on his chiseled face, but there was no humor behind it, no light behind his eyes.

"So predictable," he drawled, the words cruel and biting. "I've killed someone for attempting less."

"Is that a threat?" I asked through gritted teeth.

"No," he growled. "I just want you to know—"

"Stop trying to goad me into a response and then getting angry when I respond." I took a seat on the edge of the bed. My dress still fit me the same but it felt different on my body, which was strange. "You asked me a question. I answered. If you didn't like the answer, that's your fault, not mine. I won't shield you from the truth, Adrian, just as you haven't shielded me."

"And what truth is that?" he asked.

"Pleasure and pain are the same," I murmured. "My emotions are powerful and weak simultaneously. That I am a fool."

"You are my fool." Adrian came before me and reached down to take my face in his hands. "Is that why you refuse to let me feed from you? Because you want to inspire your father to look at you differently. You must tell him the truth, Hannah. No need to force his hand or have him change his opinion of you. You are much bolder than you initially believe."

I looked away from his penetrating blue eyes. My stomach squirmed, as though it was being pulled in multiple directions. Adrian wasn't wrong.

"What do you long for?" he asked again.

I shook my head. "I don't know," I admitted before dropping my gaze to my palms. "But I want to understand who I am, this magick inside of me. Marcella tells me I'm the only one who can learn how to control it, and yet Lizzie tells me she learned everything she knows about her magick from Thaya."

"Don't trust that witch," Adrian said, his voice a low warning.

I stood up abruptly, all but stomping to his shelf of books. I knew he referred to Thaya, not Marcella, even if he didn't clarify. "That witch is my family," I pointed out. "The only connection I have to my mother and my aunt."

"That isn't true," Adrian said. "Your magick ties you to your mother, does it not? The relationship you have with her is the same as the one you have with your magick. You aren't sure what to think of her so you don't think of her at all. She is a threat to this safe, cultivated life you live. As long as people tell you what to do, you won't have to decide for yourself. You can please everyone and avoid making decisions because you don't trust yourself. You don't trust your magick. All because you don't know your mother well enough to trust her too."

I let Adrian's words slowly sink in. I didn't understand my response to his assertion. The truth was, I didn't trust Thaya. I wasn't sure why, especially since she'd shown me where her coven was located in the forest and what sort of magick they did there. She opened herself up to me, trusting me. I needed to do the same for her.

That was the question I'd been warring with myself since the night in the forest.

"So," I said, digging my fingers in the skirts of my nightgown and slowly drawing the material of each fold out in front of me. "What do you suggest I do then, Adrian? Since you seem to know everything."

It wasn't my intention to be sarcastic, but the words came out and I couldn't swallow them back up.

"For one," Adrian reached out and took my hand, stopping me from touching my dress at all, "I believe you need to figure out what you want. You know you don't want to take over your father's business. Where does that leave you? What do you want from your life? If it's to learn this magick, then start doing that. You need no one's permission, Hannah. You are more than capable of learning on your own."

I snapped my head up and locked eyes with him, needing to see them, to check he was being sincere and wasn't simply out to make me feel better.

"I-I don't know any more than that," I admitted, looking down at my feet. "I know I want to understand my magick, but in terms of my life..." I sighed. "Lizzie knows exactly who she is. She knows exactly what she wants and she goes after it without thinking about it."

"Lizzie has no relevance to you," Adrian said, not unkindly. "She has her flaws, flaws you probably don't think she has. You need to focus on yourself and not worry about anyone else."

"Claire knew she wanted to help you." I looked at him, trying to make sense of this. "She's a girl like me, who came from where I came from. And she knew she wanted to help your cause. Lizzie knows she wants a blacksmith. She wants to learn from Thaya. I don't know what I want. I don't have that sort of passion to risk my reputation on." I threw my arms out in frustration. "I know I want to experience you feeding on me, but I am too frightened to allow you to do so! Not because I think you'll hurt me. I feel like maybe…maybe if you did, you'd be tired of me. There would be nothing left for me to offer you and you would no longer want me."

I sucked in a breath. I couldn't believe I'd just bared my soul. He stared at me, unmoving. I realized my confession could probably have ruined everything the same way him feeding on me might have.

"You foolish girl," he finally said. "Why do you assume I'd tire of you so easily?"

I tugged at my fingers, unable to meet his gaze as I tried desperately to come up with a witty explanation.

"As a woman, I was told the only thing I could offer a man was my purity, and it was important for me to retain it for my husband, the only man worthy of claiming it," I said slowly. Discussing this was difficult to do, even after the acts of intimacy we had participated in. "Once he had it though, I should expect him to stray. I should allow it because it's normal. Men aren't capable of loyalty and they have needs outside of procreation. I don't assume you and I are married, but now you have my purity, the only thing I can entice you with is my blood. If I give it to you, perhaps you will tire of me."

Darkness touched his face and he moved so quickly, he was in front of me, trapping me between the desk, leaning forward so I had to bend back.

"If that is what you were raised to believe, I implore you to understand how false it truly is," he said. "Must I repeat what I've already told you? You're the only one I've offered this to. You must understand what that means."

"Can't you say the words?" I asked in a quiet voice. I stopped fiddling with my hands, with my dress and thrust them behind my back. I tried to tighten my grip on myself so I would stop picking on anything. A current of nervous energy coursed through my body and

I cleared my throat as I paced the room. The last thing I needed was for my magick to release itself in the most inopportune way.

"Say what?" he asked. "What words do you need me to say to you?"

I looked away, trying to keep the disappointment from touching my features. Of course, he didn't know. And I shouldn't need some sort of declaration of love from Adrian to trust he loved me. At the very least, he cared more for me than he had for anyone else, as far as I knew. I should look to his actions, to the deeds he showed me to ascertain his true feelings for me. The fact he'd saved my life months ago, the fact he'd taken me in, made love to me, was willing to bond with me—surely that said enough.

And yet, I found myself wishing the words would come to him, that he'd say them not as evidence he loved me but because speaking them out loud ensured there was no room for misinterpretation.

"I don't appreciate games, Hannah," he said.

I looked up, catching his gaze. His head was tilted slightly to the side, brow furrowed, perplexed by everything.

"Tell me what is troubling you," he continued, curling a strand of errant hair behind my ear. "Tell me so I can fix it."

I smiled loosely. "Nothing is broken," I said. I stepped around his body, slowly edging my way to the door. "I assure you. And I don't play games, Adrian. I merely thought there was something you wanted to say. I won't force you to say anything you don't wish to say."

"It has nothing to do with what I want to say and what I don't," he said, following me. "It's that I don't know what you'd like to hear."

"That's just it. I don't want to hear anything you don't wish to say."

He growled, running a palm down his face. "You play games with me," he stated.

"I don't." I held up a hand. "I'm not trying to. I understand why you might think that, and I apologize. But I implore you, that's not what I'm doing." I sighed. "As lovely as this was, I should probably return home. I wouldn't want anyone to find me here with you alone."

"Your reputation would be in shambles," he agreed, though there was something that glimmered in his eyes saying he was affected by my words. I wouldn't go as far as to say they hurt him, but he reacted.

"No," I said. My hand lingered on the doorknob, and I turned to look at him over my shoulder. "It has nothing to do with me. I just know my father would react to such a thing and I wouldn't wish you to have to endure it if you don't have to. I can't predict what he will do, and I don't want anything to happen to you."

"It's cute you think you can protect me," he said, his lips curving up.

"Must I remind you I've saved your life on multiple occasions?" I teased.

Adrian said nothing in response. He placed his hand on the curve of my back and opened the door for me. "Come," he said. "I will walk you home myself. And perhaps we will do this again."

I sucked in a breath. My mouth dried at the thought of being with Adrian in this way again. My stomach turned, my pelvis throbbed even as it ached. I felt my lips twitch as I bit back a smile.

"I'd like that," I told him, locking eyes with him. I hoped he could see I meant it too. "Very much."

Adrian said nothing, but there was a sparkle in his eyes that said he was pleased by this. And his look kept me warm, even as we stepped into the frigid darkness.

CHAPTER TWENTY

Adrian

I wanted to stay, to ensure Hannah returned home safe so she wouldn't get punished for her reckless behavior. As far as I was concerned, the Pascals were still visiting and staying in the manor.

Surprisingly enough, they'd kept themselves sparse, even on Ankura. Now and then, I saw the Dwarf exploring things, buying trinkets, asking questions he shouldn't. *What is composed of the protection spell you've infused onto this stone? What are the ingredients of this love concoction?* It drew attention to himself, from both Patrol and Thaya herself.

I bristled the second I thought of the witch. I detested her with a passion. She ran through the Forest of Legend freely, doing whatever she wanted without penalty, and I was forced to hide away in a damned brothel, feeding on fucking fish to keep myself alive.

I *did* envy her freedom and her blatant disregard for the consequences. And I loathed she was trying to get Hannah to be part of it. I'd heard stories of the coven in the forest, how they feasted on magick until their source was dry, void of everything including life itself. Where the bodies went, I didn't know.

All I knew was nothing had been proven and I was still ignorant in regards to what happened to the victims. Part of me wanted to tell Hannah about it, to see if maybe she could get any information herself, but I didn't want Hannah to do something foolish.

And knowing her, she would.

Outside her home, where she'd crept in quietly and hopefully unseen, I waited until I saw the silhouette in her room. She peeked out of the curtains and gave me a small wave. My heart skipped a beat at the sight, the moon glow blanketing her face. She looked ethereal, and for a moment, I was transfixed by her sheer beauty.

I made my way back to the brothel with relative ease. The brothel itself was still in shambles, and I decided to keep from opening it tonight until it was cleaned up. The girls would appreciate the night off, and it might benefit me to have time to look more into the disappearance of my next shipment. I wasn't sure, exactly, what my next step was but I knew I had to do something.

By the time I arrived, though, the lobby was already half-filled with clients drinking to pass the time before their selected whore escorted them upstairs. I intended to keep it closed, but I couldn't do that presently. General merriment permeated the place, even though a raid had just occurred. No one seemed perturbed or concerned it would happen again. All they cared about was their pleasure, ensuring their basic needs were met after handing over a few Shellings.

A thick cloud of smoke in a corner hung over a man I'd never seen here before. It was difficult to make out who he was because the cloud clung to him and distorted his features. I liked to be privy to all clients, especially new ones. There were things I didn't quite trust about them, most especially how they heard of the brothel in the first place.

A scrawny young man bumped into me, practically skipping to follow a redhead I didn't recognize. I didn't know much about the girls here. I avoided them when I could, only discussing things with Hessie.

The smoky stranger turned at that moment, and suddenly, he was looking at me, as if he'd known I'd been there the entire time. Another couple moved past me, and I stepped out of the way so I could still be seen as I kept my eyes on the man.

Strong jaw, broad shoulders, tightly pressed mouth. I was certain this was a Blood Mage. There was something in the way he carried himself that placed them on a different level than humans. Confidence, a certainty of self.

As he made his way toward me, the smoke cleared. My eyesight kicked in. Charles…Charles Rochester? What the hell was a Lost doing in my brothel? And why wasn't he losing himself to his basic instincts? Sex and blood lingered in the air, smothering those of us with sensitive smells. Charles didn't seem perturbed in the slightest. He barely glanced at the women in their scanty attire.

Was this all because of Jessa Beckett? Was he so enamored of her?

Before I could figure it out, he was before me.

"Well?" I asked, arching a brow when he remained silent.

"I have news," he said in his low, scratchy voice. He put the rolled tobacco between his lips and tugged a long draw on it.

"Let's discuss this somewhere more private," I suggested. There were too many ears out here. It wouldn't surprise me if Diego Pascal had sent one of his cretins to spy on me, especially after the raid. He had yet to make an appearance, despite the fact the whole town seemed to know about it. Not even Hannah's father had come to the brothel to discuss it. My nose wrinkled as I led Charles up the staircase. The more I thought about it, the more I thought it odd neither man had come to see what had happened. Almost as if they already knew.

As much as I wanted to see if such a thing was true, I couldn't indulge that whim just yet, not with Charles following me up the staircase and to my office.

When we arrived, I closed the door securely behind us, locking it for good measure.

"I take it no one can hear us, even with their ears pressed against the door?" Charles asked as he made his way into the small room. "Even those with proclivities like ours?"

His hulking frame took up so much space, as did my own, that I already felt overwhelmed inside. I breezed past him, dropping gracefully into my chair and leaning back so I could look at him.

"You may speak freely," I said, folding my hands across my lap.

"The witches were gone two nights ago," Charles said.

"Gone?" I frowned. "What do you mean, gone?"

Charles picked up a map I had on my desk, narrowing his eyes at it. I knew he had been a Pyrate before he was turned, like Jonathan Nyx, which meant he would be familiar with tools of the trade. I wondered if he'd been to the Cardonian capital and if he'd traveled there on his old ship. Did this bring him fond memories? Or had he grown bitter because he couldn't travel and explore lands the way he used to? The Cardonia capital—where the Legacy lived—was all inland. There was no way Blood Mages could reach the monarchy because there was no water surrounding their castle to return to during the day. And without a body of water, the land was lethal for Blood Mages.

"I mean," he said, finally setting the map down. "They disappeared. We tend to keep an eye on them. You know, just in case."

I did know. The witches hated Blood Mages and it wasn't uncommon to hear about Blood Mage death due to magick. Of course, there was no outcry, nothing that would indicate anyone cared because no one knew Blood Mages existed. And if the witches were picking off the Lost, then Blood Mages who were created weren't going to worry because it had nothing to do with them. There was no actual threat. I wished the Lost and the witches killed each other off so I was left in peace and didn't have to worry about either of them any longer.

"Have they returned?" I asked.

Charles shook his head. "Not that I'm aware," he said. "I have a man patrolling the area, but he's reported the same thing over the last two days: the coven is empty, as though no one had been there at

138

all." He cocked his head to the side. "When are you supposed to receive your next shipment?"

"At the new moon," I said.

He nodded once. "You have a fortnight until then," he said. "The full moon's tomorrow night. Do you think you'll receive them?"

"I don't know," I admitted. "All I know is my girls went missing and my business has been raided with traces of magick. Perhaps if I could trace the magick—"

"You can."

I frowned. "What?"

"I know someone who's able to do just that," Charles said. "She can take magick and do a ritualistic ceremony before coming up with who the magick belongs to."

I sat in my chair and leaned back, staring up at the ceiling as casually as I could. Was it possible or was Charles lying? If it was the latter, I didn't understand why he would lie in the first place. It made no sense.

I wished Hannah was here. She could tell me the truth.

"Who is she?" I asked instead.

"I won't tell you her name or anything about her unless you ask for her," Charles said. "If anyone found out what she could do..." He let his voice trail off, midnight-blue eyes hard and narrowed. "Though, I suppose I don't have to tell you. You already know."

"I won't tolerate games, Charles," I spat, turning to face him. I drew to my natural height, towering over him by inches. He didn't flinch under the action but his eyes flickered to the door before returning to my face. "If you know someone who can decipher what magick belongs to whom, you will tell me who it is."

"Not until you do something for me first," Charles said.

"And what's that?" I asked.

"You will let my men feed on the Sirens," he said.

I jerked my head back, surprised by the request. "Excuse me?" I asked. I couldn't have heard him correctly.

Charles looked away. There was discomfort on his tight features, and I realized he didn't wish to ask me this at all.

"My men," he said. "I need them to feed from the fish folk."

"Tell me why," I demanded to know.

Charles's jaw tightened. For a moment, I thought he'd refuse to tell me, simply insist on it not being my business. And unfortunately, I would have agreed to it. It might have placed the girls in danger, but I needed to figure out what was going on and what had happened to the other girls. If that meant letting the Lost feed from the girls here, so be it.

"I found a body," he said. He still wouldn't look away. His garbled voice was strained, and I realized this was difficult for him to admit. "Close to the Black Shore. A day ago. Looked decimated. Unrecognizable. I couldn't even smell what she was. I know Patrol isn't aware of her, but it's only a matter of time."

"And you believe your men were responsible?" I asked.

"My men are a lot more civil than people believe," he said defensively. I waited. Charles's face darkened and he walked away from me until he stood behind the chair positioned in front of my desk. "I don't know if they are or not. But just in case, I figured I would try to stop this from happening again."

"I want to see the body," I said.

"What? Why?"

"I want to see the body," I repeated. "I will agree, under my terms, to let your men feed on Sirens of my choosing. All of my rules must be followed for this to work. In exchange, you will arrange a meeting with this woman who can trace magick, and you will allow me to see the body you found."

Charles searched my face, trying to decipher why I would agree to such a thing. But it didn't matter. He was forced to agree. We both knew it.

"Fine." He stuck out his hand. "We have an accord."

I shook his hand, smirking. "Good. Bring me the body." I paused. "Who is the woman who can trace magick?"

He loosed a breath and glanced out the window. "Jessa Beckett."

CHAPTER TWENTY-ONE

Hannah

I woke late the next morning, my body still sore after everything Adrian and I had done. Now I was alone, I could reflect on what had happened.

I took a seat at my bureau and slowly removed my nightgown so I could view myself stark naked. Instead of shying away from my body, I made myself look. I took in the marks Adrian left on my neck in his passion, took in the graceful curve of my shoulders, the swell of my breasts, the softness of my stomach and the fullness of my thighs. I stood up and turned so I could do the same thing to my back, my buttocks, and my legs.

Being with Adrian intimately wasn't something I'd expected. It was the first choice I'd made on my own. As I looked at myself in the mirror, taking myself in and noticing every imperfection about myself, I realized I didn't regret it.

I slipped on a silky robe, the thin material coating my naked frame from the cold, before reaching for my barely used powder and brush. I might have passed on having Adrian feed on me, but I could still hide the marks on my neck with the tools I did possess. By the time I finished, they were barely visible. I smiled with pride, set the brush down, and began to fiddle with my hair.

I felt older, wiser. It was silly. Hours had passed, nothing more, and yet, it was as though the entire world shifted. I saw things differently. I was a new person. When I finished doing my hair—I left it down, with small, tiny braids weaved with little vines of flowers—I pushed myself up. As sore as I was, each time my pelvis throbbed, my lips curved up. It was a reminder of what had happened last night, something reminding me it wasn't a dream.

Adrian and I had been together more than once. In truth, I wanted to do it again, but I wasn't sure how to go about doing such a thing, about initiating it. Part of me wanted him to chase after me. The thrill of power that teased me during our time together was something I wanted more of. It made me feel bold, like I could do anything I set my mind to.

The sash of my robe fell open as I made my way to my wardrobe. Instead of tying it back up, I let my body be displayed. I wasn't ashamed of myself. Certainly, there were flaws I knew I possessed, but they didn't matter. They didn't detract from my desirability.

Such a difference I felt about myself. Under normal circumstances, I would tie my sash back up, my cheeks would turn red, and I would lecture myself for believing I was perfect. Now, I embraced it. If Adrian could want me the way he did, surely it meant something. He had women throwing themselves at his feet constantly. The fact he'd chosen me had to say something.

I reached the wardrobe and opened the wooden door. My eyes rested on the numerous dresses filling the space. I wasn't sure what I wanted to wear. I tugged on the skirts of a few before letting them fall back into place. The clothes Adrian lent me months ago were still tucked in the corner, and I contemplated throwing them on for the day.

I knew I wouldn't. My father would question my attire—if I saw him at all today—and I didn't want to draw any unwanted attention to myself.

Instead, I found a rose-gold dress and decided I would wear it. It was simple without being overtly restricting, and I could put it on without Roseanna's assistance. Once again, I must have slept too late for her to be here when I woke up, though I knew if I called her, she would come immediately.

I didn't want to do that. I found I didn't mind this quiet time of doing things on my own.

After pulling on the dress and ensuring my hair was relatively neat, I made my way out of the room and down the stairs. My first intended destination was the kitchen. I hoped one of the cooks would be lingering about and I would be able to get a late breakfast, something that would fill my belly, when I heard voices from my father's study.

I tilted my head to the side as I slowed my steps. I didn't recall Father having any guests recently, and he rarely met at home for things related to his business. The few times Adrian had stopped by were unexpected and uncommon. My father tried to keep both lives separate if he could.

"…don't know what's going on with her," my sister's voice said. "Is that why you've come? She confided in you about something?"

"I just…I'm concerned."

I knew that voice. Brendan Pickard. What was he doing here?

At that moment, a maid stepped out of the library, nearly bumping into me. Her arms were occupied by a bunch of dirty plates, and I realized she must have come from my father's room. He must have eaten his dinner in his room, though why he would do so, I couldn't say.

I didn't care enough to try to figure it out.

Lizzie and Brendan were having a heated discussion. I wondered if he'd come back to talk about their former relationship and what he could do to win her back. I shouldn't listen in. This wasn't my place, and it wasn't right for me to purposefully eavesdrop on a private conversation. I considered continuing, pretending I hadn't heard anything in the first place, when more of their conversation drifted toward me from behind the thick, heavy door.

"Davenport saw her with Adrian Blood a couple of months back," Brendan said. His voice was muffled but I could pick up the words easily. "Alone. At night."

They weren't discussing their relationship. They were discussing *me*.

I dug my nails into my palms. My first instinct was to rush in there and demand an explanation. Who did they think they were, discussing me like I was a rambunctious child they needed to fix?

I knew I should leave them be, pretend their words didn't affect me. But I couldn't let it go. Brendan and Lizzie hadn't spoken directly in months. Something must have triggered this. Something I had done. And I needed to know what it was.

I glanced up and down the hall. When I was assured I was truly alone, I ducked into the library. There was a place tucked in the left corner of the room where if I placed my ear on the wall, the conversation flitted in from the study and I could hear every word as though I was right there in the room with them.

I made my way through the stacks of books and into the corner. I pushed a small table out of the way and positioned my body just so, tucking myself against the wall and pressing my ear against the wall.

"…going through something she's keeping tightly veiled," Lizzie said. There was a tremor in her voice, indicating she was worried about me. "Brendan, I want to help her, but she won't even let me in. I feel completely powerless to do anything. I can't— I can't help her. And I've always been the one to help her."

"Does this have anything to do with Adrian Blood?" Brendan asked. Curious. Not quite judgmental or critical. There was a pause.

"Adrian Blood?" Lizzie repeated, slightly guarded and almost protective. I appreciated Lizzie's need to defend me if she felt she needed to, even if it was to Brendan.

"Don't make such a face, Lizzie. You forget I can read you like a book. Don't pretend like you didn't notice it too."

"What face are you talking about? I'm not making a face."

"Yes, you are," he insisted. "You're doing that thing, where you wrinkle your brow and your nose at the same time. I know what that means, okay?"

"And what does it mean?"

"It means you know exactly what I'm talking about and you're trying to protect your sister, that's what. And I get it. Trust me, I want to protect Davenport from all his bull-headed mistakes—and, trust me, he makes plenty of them. I just…is she okay?"

"Why do you ask?" Lizzie's voice had gone quiet, reserved.

"Adrian Blood doesn't have the best reputation, Lizzie. I mean, for god's sake, he runs a brothel. You know he has more experience than she ever could. If she isn't careful, she could ruin any prospects she might have. If she takes up with the likes of him, she's throwing her future away. Her actions…they're rash. Completely unlike her. I just…I want to know if she's okay."

Lizzie sighed. She murmured something in a low voice, one I couldn't pick up. I pressed my ear even harder into the wood.

"You know," Brendan said. "I had this picture of us, the four of us. We were all married together, on the same day. You and me, your sister and Henry. And we were happy."

"Yes, well, that didn't happen." Lizzie's voice wasn't exactly cold, but it wasn't indulgent either. "Maybe if things were different, maybe if she and Henry were still together…" Her voice trailed off. I imagined her pacing the length of the room, imagined her hands going to her hair and her fingers deftly braiding her locks the way she always did when something heavy was on her mind. "But they aren't."

"Lizzie, do you believe Adrian Blood is only with Hannah because of her…because of what she can do?"

My eyebrows lifted and I jerked my head back from the wall, as though my skin had been scalded. How was it possible Brendan knew about my magick? If someone overheard, they might turn me in for the money. Patrol had set up a fund that rewarded people for turning over those with magickal abilities, and it incentivized even families to cross each other for financial gain. I thought Brendan had been the person to implement the system, though now…

If he knew about me, I was certain he knew about Lizzie. That made sense, considering everyone believed the reason their betrothal disintegrated was because of his tightly laced beliefs and how Lizzie completely contradicted those beliefs.

But what if…what if it wasn't true? What if they broke their betrothal for a different reason?

I held my breath, still waiting for Lizzie's answer.

"I don't know why Adrian Blood wants my sister, Brendan," she said. "Though it wouldn't surprise me if she knows he is using her for some purpose of his own. She tries to hide her emotions, but it is easy to read her. I don't even need my gift most of the time. Thaya says it's important to keep in practice, to use it always, but Hannah and I always promised we wouldn't. I'm not sure what the right thing is anymore. Thaya says we must deceive those we love to protect them from wickedness, but what if she's wrong? Shouldn't I let her explore her feelings for him the same way I did with you?" A pause. "Thaya says Adrian is a threat to her, to her gifts, but I…I've seen the way he looks at her. I know something inside of him genuinely cares for her. I know that sounds nonsensical, but it's true."

"I believe you, Lizzie. If Hannah can obtain affection from the likes of Davenport, I know she can do it from anyone. But that doesn't mean he doesn't pose a threat to her. Tell me, do you trust your aunt?"

I caught my breath. My heart pounded. I needed to know the answer. Needed to understand—

"Well, well, well, Ms. Walker. I didn't think I'd find you tucked in a corner, eavesdropping." Diego Pascal emerged, clicking his tongue against the back of his teeth, masking any sort of response Lizzie might have regarding Thaya. "I'm glad to have found you. I've been looking for you everywhere."

CHAPTER TWENTY-TWO

Hannah

I closed my eyes in disbelief. Surely I was dreaming. Diego Pascal wasn't here, didn't have a smarmy smile on his face, and hadn't been looking for me, of all people. I'd managed to avoid him mostly, what with him preparing for his upcoming nuptials to Everly. It was wrong, of course, but I reveled in his distraction. It meant I could move more freely around the manor without needing to worry about suspicious eyes following me, or people slipping out of the house and reporting on my actions.

Even now, I could still feel the press of the blade on my cheek as he'd threatened me that night. Luckily, it hadn't scarred. No one noticed. No one save for Adrian.

"Shall I inform them you're listening in on their conversation?" Diego asked. It was odd how a man with such a musical voice could inflict such fear. Even now, my heartbeat pounded against my chest like someone trapped in a room, desperate to get out.

"Mr. Pascal," I said slowly, hoping he couldn't detect the tremor in my tone. "Who am I to tell you to do anything? I would never assume I have any sort of power over you. You will do as you please."

The corners of his lips sliced up, but the man before me wasn't smiling. His cold, dark eyes took me in slowly, trying to spot something, though I wasn't sure what. My back was pressed against the wall and I could no longer hear Brendan or Lizzie. Whether they were still discussing my romantic life with Adrian was anyone's guess; however, I hoped not. I hoped they had changed the subject so Diego Pascal couldn't hear a single word.

"You seem very clever, Ms. Walker," he said, "but you aren't. You run with wolves, and eventually, you're going to get eaten by one."

"Are you pretending to worry about my well-being?" I asked, shoulders hunched up. My position was vulnerable, him towering over me, forcing me to press against the wall behind me, but somehow, I still managed to find the confidence to look him in the eye and prevent myself from stammering.

"Would you believe me if I said yes?" Diego cocked his head to the side, lips curling into a smirk. "Tell me, Ms. Walker, why are you so terribly interested in whatever story you're listening to? Perhaps the two former lovers are discussing something that has nothing to do with you. I would be remiss if I let your innocent ears listen to something too intimate. And I'm certain you wouldn't want to overstep and invade your sister's privacy."

I wrinkled my nose. Lizzie had no qualms about listening in on *my* conversations. She had no problem using her magick on me, even if it was only one time. As far as I was concerned, she wasn't allowed the privacy she expected, not anymore.

His eyes dropped to my neck and narrowed. I tried to school my face into a look of passivity. But he wouldn't look elsewhere, even as the footsteps of Brendan and Lizzie faded from the room.

They were gone, leaving just me and Diego together…alone.

This was not good. I didn't trust Diego Pascal. I hadn't trusted him since I met him, and since he had come to my home as a guest, he hadn't given me a reason to change my mind about him. The more I learned about him, the more I realized just how dangerous he was. If someone like Adrian Blood could be wary of him, that meant something. I had to always be on my guard around him.

"Something is different about you, Hannah," he said, gazing back up at me. The corners of his lips tilted up and his eyes sparkled with amusement. "It shows on your body. Tell me, have you been intimate with Adrian Blood?"

I tried to suppress the fear and panic building. How could he possibly suspect that? Had he seen the marks on my neck? I knew I'd used an excessive amount of powder, but I didn't think it was obvious. And even if it was, I didn't think it possible he could tell what exactly was underneath the powder.

"You have, haven't you?" he said. His smile widened, turning smug, and he lifted his arm and placed it over my head, leaning forward, caging me in like an animal. "Well, this is an interesting turn of events."

"I'm not sure what you mean." I ducked under his arm and made my way from him. I passed the coffee table, which still held books I had yet to read. I picked one up so it didn't look as if I'd been eavesdropping, even though I was quite certain Diego knew what I was doing.

"I think you know exactly what I mean," he said. It wasn't long before he pushed himself in front of me, blocking me from leaving. His movements were practically feline, and when he stepped, he made no sound. I wouldn't be surprised if part of him was as supernatural as my magick or Adrian's bloodlust. "You've crossed a line with Adrian Blood. The two of you are intimate..." His eyes burned my face like he could see through my skin and blood and bones straight to my soul. "He cares for you."

"Adrian cares for no one except himself," I snapped. This was a reactionary response, but one I didn't quite believe. I knew Adrian cared for me—but that didn't mean Diego had to know.

"That is why he lingers, isn't it?" Diego said, bringing his index finger to his chin and staring off at the rows of books behind me. He ignored my claim, dismissing it as false without saying a word. "This is good news, yes?"

He seemed to be talking more to himself than to me at this point, which was fine with me. I just wanted to slip by him and return to my room. Let him think whatever he wanted and do what he felt compelled to do.

I smoothed the wrinkles in my skirt—I had already twisted and turned the material in my hands so much, I doubted removing the wrinkles was possible at this point—but it gave me a task to do with my hands. I edged around him, hoping he wouldn't notice as he seemed too consumed by his thoughts,

I was mistaken. His hand shot out, fingers coiled around my wrist. "Where do you think you're going? That's very rude, Hannah," he chided, pulling me toward him. "You know, we aren't finished with our discussion. Not until I say we are." His fingers squeezed my skin and I knew I was going to have bruises after this encounter.

"What do you want from me?" I asked. My teeth clamped together to prevent him from hearing the pain he inflicted on me.

"Don't you get it?" Diego said, pulling me closer to him. My chest was nearly pressed against his. The only reason we weren't touching was that I arched my back from preventing it in the first place. "If Adrian Blood cares for you, you are the key to everything."

He wasn't making any sense. At least, not to me. I was a key? Key to what? What was he going on about?

"Do you realize how much power I'd have over him if I could use you against him?" A wild flame danced in Diego's eyes, making him appear more unhinged than I'd ever seen him. I needed to get out of there, and soon, or else I didn't know what might happen.

"Adrian would never…." My hands instinctively fumbled over my brow, as if trying to brush nonexistent hair out of my face, then dropped back at my sides. Magick thrummed in me, reminding me I could use it should I need to. But if I did that, he'd know what I was, what I was capable of. And that would put me in greater danger than I already seemed to be in with him.

Unless you kill him, my internal voice pointed out.

I immediately banished the thought. I was still reeling over Pepper's death—the death I'd caused. The worst part of it all was I didn't regret it. Not at all. Because if I hadn't done what I did, Adrian would be a pile of ash, lost to the wind.

And I couldn't have that. Not if I could do something to save him. And I wasn't a killer. At least, I didn't label myself as such.

But the fact I'd killed someone and would do it again if I needed to scared me more than I was willing to admit. It was part of me, something out of my control. And I hated being out of control.

"You're a fool," Diego sneered.

I balked at the words he used so casually. Adrian constantly said it to me, but there was affection behind it, something almost endearing. It was never used as an insult.

"Adrian would do anything for you." Diego reached out and I leaned back, trying to keep myself away from his touch. But I was trapped, pressed against this bookcase with no means of escape. His finger pressed against my cheek, in the exact place he'd sliced through months ago.

A shudder ripped down my spine. Diego's lips curved up, amused by my reaction to him. Like he knew he had this power over me. Like he would never relinquish it, no matter what.

I hated him, in that moment.

My magick burned and it took everything in me to keep myself from lashing out. I wanted to smother the smirk off his pretty face, inflict the pain he so rightly deserved since he seemed to have no issue doing it to anyone else.

"You'll deliver a message to Adrian for me," he said.

"Will I?" I couldn't help but bite back. I wasn't sure it was the smartest response, considering he could harm me, could pierce my skin and make me bleed. Could hurt me through hurting Adrian or even Everly. I couldn't risk angering him since I wasn't sure how he'd lash out. He was unpredictable like fire, which made him all the more dangerous.

"You will," he agreed, humor lighting up his dark eyes, lips still curved up. He was handsome, but an abhorrent person. Everything in me shriveled in disgust. "You will."

His arrogance was infuriating, and I wanted to be the one to strip him of it. And yet, we both knew I'd do no such thing. I would do as he asked because it meant helping Adrian, doing what I could to protect him.

"What's the message?" I demanded. I loathed this game he seemed to revel in playing, wishing he would just stop it.

Diego's face lit up with a brilliant smile. It completely contradicted his cruelty, and it was easy to forget he wasn't the sort of man to cross. Even I sometimes needed to be reminded he could kill me if he chose to.

"I'm glad to see you've come around," he said. "I'm curious to know—are you aware of the missing girls Adrian collects every month to work at his brothel?"

I carefully schooled my face into a look of innocence. "What are you talking about?"

Diego's lips curved upward even more. "Feigning innocence?" he teased. "If only I believed you...but I don't. See, I believe you know about the Sirens. I believe Adrian has informed you about much more than he should have. And that is all right, Hannah, because your knowledge is useful for me. If Adrian is willing to risk his secrets to you, it must mean you know what he is, that you're aware he's a monster. And if you know that, then you must know someone created him, yes? I need you to inform him that should he go another month without following through with our deal, I will kill you."

I blinked. There were a lot of ways I thought the conversation might end but threatening my life wasn't one of them. I was still a Walker. I was still my father's daughter. How dare he threaten me in my own home. Was he simply that arrogant?

"Adrian was created for one purpose and one purpose alone," Diego continued. "Should he refrain from fulfilling that purpose, I have no qualms about killing you slowly in front of him before ending his life as well. I am a very important man, and too many pieces are at play to suffer any mistakes. Do I make myself clear?"

I wanted to spit in his face. I wanted to shoot magick at him and paralyze him. Instead, I managed to force myself to say, "Crystal."

He grinned, tapping my face with his palm, almost like he was slapping me but not quite. "Good," he said. "I'll see you soon. And, Hannah, remember, I have men watching you all the time. Don't think I won't know should you try to disobey me. The same goes for Adrian." He stepped back and left the library without turning to look at me.

Only when I heard the door click shut did I finally find my breath. I let out a frustrated roar. My hands slammed on the surface of the coffee table and whipped the stack of books off it. They went crashing to the floor. Magick sparked out of me, but I managed to direct it into my palms instead of anywhere else. I caught my temper after a moment and shook my head.

Then I stood up. I had no idea what I was going to do. I needed to help Adrian get his shipment, but I feared our investigation was stagnant. How could we move forward without some kind of lead? I dropped to my knees in a huff, trying to think but couldn't come up with anything.

A fortnight would pass quickly. If we didn't have something, Adrian and I would perish. I couldn't let that happen. No matter what it cost.

CHAPTER TWENTY-THREE

Hannah

I didn't know how I managed to sleep that night, but I did. Until the presence of someone in my room woke me up.

It was such a strange sensation, being woken up by silence, by something that felt different even if nothing appeared as such. There was no noise, no shuffling across the floor, no opening drawers or bumping into the bed. But I knew someone was there.

I sat up in bed, fully awake, and waited. I knew whoever was there had seen me move and knew I was no longer sleeping. What they chose to do with that information was anyone's guess at this point. Were they going to attack me? Had Diego Pascal sent someone to kill me? I didn't think so; I hadn't even informed Adrian of his threat, but maybe it didn't matter. Maybe killing me would be a threat enough.

"Hannah?"

Adrian's familiar voice caused my heart to squeeze together painfully. I leapt from the bed, twisting my ankle on the sheets and falling forward. Luckily, I managed to catch myself just in time. I kicked the sheets off my foot and stood, only to find him right there, reaching toward me to offer his assistance.

"You are troubled," he stated as he placed his hands on my waist, granting me stability.

I brushed stray strands of hair out of my face before nodding once. "To be fair, I didn't expect you to show up in my bedroom unannounced."

He tilted his head to the side as his eyes flashed with amusement. His lips remained stoic as if he wanted to smile but there was something more serious on his mind.

"I must discuss something with you," he said. "It's important."

I nodded. That much was obvious. As much as I wanted to think Adrian was consumed by his passion for me, I wasn't a fool. I knew there was more to this.

"Would you like to sit down?" There was nowhere for him to do so save for the chair at my bureau or the edge of my bed. I took a seat on the end of my bed, folding my hands in my lap. My body was tense with confusion, my magick crackling around my hands and fingers, as though my body was preparing for battle. I loosed a shaky breath and hoped Adrian didn't pick it up. He followed me to where I was and smoothly sat on the bed, careful to put enough space between us so we wouldn't be touching.

I wasn't sure if that indicated a bad sign or not. Perhaps he was here to tell me what a mistake we made by becoming intimate. It would explain why he hadn't swooped me in his arms and kissed me upon seeing me. Or perhaps I was being too romantic for my own good. I had told him I didn't think anything would come of our coupling, and I meant it. He was the one who insisted I now belonged to him. He was the one who said he wanted to bond with me in a way that was much stronger than marriage.

"There's a body," he said. "I believe it's one of the girls I was supposed to have received at the New Moon."

My brows shot up and relief filled my body. This wasn't going to be a discussion about us, about our relationship or the intimacy that came from it. It was going to be about the Sirens.

Instantly, guilt overtook my relief. Someone had died, and there was a good chance it was one of the Sirens. They'd been brought here through no fault of their own, and one of them had suffered a tragedy. That was terrible, and here I was, soothed because Adrian hadn't told me he didn't want me.

What was wrong with me? I ran my fingers down the length of my skirt. The rose-gold color appeared flat after my encounter with Diego Pascal, but now Adrian was here, it was picking up its color once more.

"Do we know how she died?" I forced myself to ask. I knew he was waiting on some kind of response from me.

"Magick."

My eyes widened as I carefully took in his face. It wasn't as though I didn't believe him. Rather, I wasn't sure what to make of it. How could he know it was magick?

"Someone delivered the body to me," he said. "Charles Rochester."

I frowned. My hands stilled in my lap. Charles Rochester? The name sounded familiar, though I couldn't remember why.

"Isn't he some sort of Pyrate?" I finally asked, tilting my head to the side.

"Was," Adrian corrected.

"He has died?" I asked. I racked my brain for any mention of him, any memory that might have been touched by his presence. "He hasn't been spotted for months, years, possibly. I assumed he was somewhere else, on another of his grand adventures."

"He's closer than you might think," Adrian said.

I rolled my eyes and crossed my arms over my chest. "Must you play games with me?" I asked.

"I want to know the relationship he had with your cousin, Jessa Beckett," Adrian said.

It hit me like a slap in the face, like a blade slicing across my skin. Suddenly, I remembered exactly who Charles Rochester was. He was Jessa's downfall, her ruin. It had been two years ago when Jessa was seventeen, my age. I didn't know why the memories hadn't come easily. Perhaps I'd buried them away the same way I was sure Jessa had.

"They were lovers," I said, looking back at Adrian. "She was in love with him. I'm not sure how he felt about her. One day, he simply vanished without warning." I cleared my throat. "He broke her heart and didn't say a word." I stood up and took a step forward. "Why? Why are you concerned with my cousin and a Pyrate?"

"That Pyrate is a Lost," he said. He moved off the bed as well, watching me.

"Lost?" I frowned. "You mean he's a Blood Mage."

Adrian wrinkled his nose and brushed past me. His fingers tugged at his blond hair and he took a few paces, back rigid. He turned back to face me, and I could see from the expression on his face he was trying to figure out how to explain it to me.

I huffed, crossing my arms over my chest. I wished to inform him I wasn't as dense as he treated me, but I didn't want to agitate him or give him some sort of excuse to distract himself with. Instead, I tilted my chin down and waited.

"Blood Mages are created by a single Creator," Adrian said. "I didn't exist before I was brought into this world. I was…concocted, I suppose. Charles Rochester, on the other hand, wasn't. He was turned by a Blood Mage, thus becoming one himself. However, there's a line between what I am and what Charles is. He's more…animalistic, giving in to more basic instincts. He doesn't have the same rational thought he once had when he was alive."

I let his words sink in before I said anything, trying to understand before asking something that revealed my ignorance.

"Wait," I said slowly. "You said he mentioned Jessa? That's how you know about her?"

Adrian nodded.

"Huh." I frowned.

"You seem…confused," he stated. There was a sparkle of amusement in his eyes, though he wasn't laughing at me.

Not yet, anyway.

"I just…you said he doesn't have rational thought," I said, curling errant hair behind my ear. "Then how could he possibly remember her?"

Adrian opened his mouth before shutting it. He cocked his head to the side, staring over my shoulder, out of my window.

"Who told you those were the differences anyway?" I asked.

"I've seen the Lost with my own eyes," he said.

"Perhaps some are more animalistic during their transition," I allowed, picking at a loose thread on the comforter. "But perhaps they evolve after a certain period. Perhaps they are more like you than you care to acknowledge."

Adrian snapped his head to the side, teeth clenched, but he didn't deny it.

"I mean no offense, Adrian," I said. "I'm merely trying to understand—"

"We're losing focus," he said. "You say Charles and Jessa were lovers and Charles brought about her downfall?"

I nodded. "Uncle barely speaks to Jessa, he's disappointed with her. At least Father still treats Lizzie like she belongs to our family."

"And that is why you feel so much pressure to do as he bids you to," Adrian murmured. It felt like he was talking to himself rather than to me.

I wasn't sure what sort of response to give him, so I said nothing.

"Will you meet with us?" he asked me.

My eyes darted to my bedroom door as if expecting someone to burst through and stop this conversation dead in its tracks.

"When?" I asked in a low voice. It was too easy to listen to conversations, even behind closed doors. I couldn't risk anyone overhearing us.

"Tomorrow night," he said. "There's magick on the body, and I intend to see who it leads to. I believe if I find that out, I'll figure out who stole my shipment."

"Good," I said, nodding once.

Adrian's eyes narrowed and his fingers found the underside of my chin. He tilted my face up so my eyes were locked with his. His icy blue stare scanned me up and down, taking in every nuance on my face. What he was searching for, I had no idea. I remained still, letting him devour me, hoping to control my rapidly beating heart and failing miserably.

"What aren't you telling me?" he asked. "Something's happened."

"I—"

"Don't lie to me," he said. I knew that would be the only warning he would give me.

I sucked in a breath, hoping to be subtle about it. As much as I wanted to tell Adrian everything, I didn't want Adrian to do something rash, like attack Diego simply for threatening me.

"Diego Pascal wants me to deliver a message to you," I said calmly as my hands began to pull and tug. It was all I could do to keep myself from releasing the magick inside.

Adrian said nothing, though I noticed the tic in his jaw, the way he tucked his chin down as a means for me to continue. Cold fury seemed to sweep through him, touching his angled features. He was probably doing everything he could to keep from extracting his fangs, to keep from reacting. Since I was only the messenger, I appreciated his effort.

"Did he...did he harm you?" he asked, his voice catching.

I shook my head. "He cornered me in the library," I replied. "Touched my cheek where he..." I didn't finish the sentence. I didn't need to. "He told me..." I hesitated. Did I need to tell Adrian everything? He already knew how dangerous Diego Pascal was. He was already stressed enough as it was. I had my magick; I should be able to take care of this myself.

And yet, I couldn't bring myself to lie to him. I didn't want to keep something from him that could turn up and ruin whatever trust we'd created with each other.

"Hannah." Adrian's voice was low, but there was a note of insistence. "Please."

I hesitated. "He told me he would kill me if you didn't receive the next delivery." I stood up from the edge of the bed and brushed past him, and Adrian caught my wrist and prevented me from moving any farther. "He said your creator would be displeased, that this task is the sole purpose of why you are here in the first place, and if you can't do it, he will find ways to motivate you to listen, using me."

Adrian's hand never left my wrist. With my free one, I reached out tentatively until I cupped his cheek with my palm. It felt strange to be so intimate in my room. There was meaning behind every touch, more so than usual.

"You know I will never let anything happen to you," he said softly. "I will protect you with all of me."

I nodded, unable to find the words.

"And I will do everything in my power to protect you," I said, hoping he trusted me, hoping he understood.

Adrian's other hand held my waist, pulling me into his lap. Without saying anything, he touched his lips to mine in a tender kiss. It always surprised me he could be gentle. At that moment, the door to my bedroom burst open.

In walked my father, and he didn't look happy.

CHAPTER TWENTY-FOUR

Hannah

For one sheer second, I saw my downfall from the outside looking in. I didn't even think to pull myself away from Adrian's embrace, too shocked to move let alone protect my reputation. We'd been caught red-handed. My father was supposed to be in a meeting on the other side of the manor.

"What the devil is the meaning of this?" he demanded. Adrian slowly pulled me off his lap and we stood and turned towards my father. His eyes were only on me, his focus hard like stone. To him, Adrian wasn't even in the room.

Until Adrian positioned himself in front of me, protecting me from my father's ire. I squeezed my eyes shut, then popped one open in time to see my father curl his fingers into tight, knuckled fists and take a threatening step toward him.

I couldn't see what Adrian did because his back was facing me, but I knew it was something that indicated he wasn't going to move. And why would he? Adrian was a Blood Mage. My father was a human who had power but not necessarily over him. Not the way Diego Pascal did.

"Well?" my father continued. "Would you care to explain what is going on?"

"I think you know exactly what's going on," Adrian said smoothly.

I wanted to hit him. His arrogant tone wasn't helping, and I didn't have to see his face to know he was smirking.

"I want to hear it from her. From my daughter."

Adrian didn't move. I honestly thought he believed my father was going to do something bad to me and he wasn't about to let that happen. If I didn't insert myself into this scenario now, I wasn't sure how this was going to end.

I had to fix it before either one of them did something they would later regret.

"Father," I said, slowly stepping around Adrian so I could stand by his side. "Adrian and I...the thing is, you see...Adrian and I..."

"Are engaged," Adrian finished.

My father blinked. Any anger he might have felt toward the Blood Mage was overcome by confusion. "Excuse me?" he asked, turning his attention back to me. It was like he didn't believe a word coming from Adrian. As he said, he needed to hear it from me, or it was a lie.

I glanced over at Adrian. I had no idea what he was doing. Out of all the things he could have said, the last thing I expected was him binding himself to me so intimately, so willingly. I didn't understand. Why would he do that? What was he playing at?

When I returned my gaze to my father, he wrinkled his brow, silently asking me for some sort of answer. "Y-yes," I said slowly. I had to trust Adrian, even if I wasn't sure what his plan was. "Father, I-I apologize for how unorthodox this is, but Adrian and I are engaged."

"You can't be serious." My father shifted his weight from one foot to the other. He placed his hands on his hips and I could see the tension radiating from his body. I was surprised he didn't combust from building up the energy inside of him.

"Hannah. We discussed this. You know what he is. You know what he's capable of." He shook his head and began to pace the length of my room, his gaze going to the floor instead of remaining on me. "No. I won't approve of this union."

"There's nothing you can do or say that will stop me from being with your daughter," Adrian said before I could say anything. His words were clipped, laced with a warning tone. Then, as an afterthought, with a small hint of smugness, he added, "Sir."

I closed my eyes, a light wince caressing my features before I opened my eyes again and sat back on the edge of the bed.

"What has gotten into you, Hannah?" my father demanded, completely ignoring Adrian. "I expect this sort of reckless behavior from your sister, but from you? He's a monster. He's a wicked man who will claim your heart as his before crushing it in his hand. It will be nothing more than ash when he is through with it. There will be no pieces for you to stitch back together—if he doesn't kill you first."

Without warning, Adrian let out a growl. His eyes turned icy as he narrowed them on my father.

"I ask you to refrain from lying about me to my fiancée," Adrian said tightly. I could feel how taut his body was, even though we still had yet to touch. "I would never hurt her."

"You wouldn't be able to resist her if she was bleeding from a damned paper cut!" my father roared, whirling around and facing him completely. His arms hulked down at his sides, his shoulders hunched over his body, and his face flooded with blood, making the pallor of his skin and bright red color. He looked...unhinged. I didn't think I had ever seen him this angry. "You would feed on her until you drank every last drop from her, and from there, you would either let her die or you would turn her into one of you."

Adrian's nostrils flared and he took a step forward in one graceful sweep. How someone so beautiful could look so lethal at the same time, I had no idea. I leaned back, careful not to touch him, though I wasn't sure what his intention was with my father. Surely, he wouldn't harm him.

"Don't deign to know what I'm capable of," Adrian said slowly, each word clipped with its warning. "I would never harm your daughter. I love her."

He said the words...to my father. I widened my eyes, ready to slap Adrian, ready to demand he direct those words to me, for once and for all. This wasn't how I wanted to hear his confession. This wasn't how I wanted to deepen the intimacy between us.

Warmth bloomed in my chest like the first flower feeling the warmth of the spring sunshine. My lips curled up into a smile I couldn't fight off, even if I wanted to. I ducked my chin, forcing the hair not twisted into braids to fall on my face. I hoped it walled off the expression I currently had from my father. I didn't think he'd be too pleased to see I was delighted by the words Adrian had casually flung out during their conversation, even if the context was less than ideal.

He loves me. He loves me.

My father burst into laughter that seemed to bubble deep within his stomach. He threw his head back, arms wrapped around his stocky frame as some sort of support.

"You what?" he demanded between said laughter. His cheeks were still red, but now, it was due to his clear amusement rather than anything else. "You love her? Do you even know what love is?"

"Father." It took me a moment to realize I had spoken, but when I did, I relaxed my shoulders and set my narrowed gaze at the man who raised me. "I won't have you treating Adrian thusly."

My father looked at me like he hadn't seen me at all until this very moment. The silence between the three of us was palpable. I could slice into it with a dagger should I want to.

I wanted nothing more than to press my face against Adrian's back, having him shield me from my father and his looming presence. All my life, I had never been intimidated by him. And now? Now I realized why he was able to even acquire Adrian's compliance in their mutual agreement of protection in exchange for exuberant fees. He was intimidating when he wanted to be.

I had never seen this side of him, and now that I had...

"You don't know what you're saying," my father said firmly. There was something in his voice, something only I seemed to be able to pick up. A flicker, revealing his true disappointment with me.

I tried not to be affected by it. I tried not to feel guilty as it snaked around my heart and clenched it tightly in its grasp. But even I couldn't help it. The last thing I ever wanted to do was disappoint him. Besides Lizzie, he was the only immediate family I had. As much as I loved my cousins, my uncle, they weren't my sisters and my uncle wasn't my father. And to see Father frown as he took me in, a look of complete disapproval on his face as he rested his eyes on me rather than Lizzie, it hurt.

As painful as this feeling was, however, I couldn't give in. I had to stand my ground. I couldn't let him manipulate my emotions to do his bidding.

"I know exactly what I'm saying, Father," I said slowly. With each word, my heart increased in beats. There was a tremor in my voice, one I wondered if he could detect. Did he know how difficult this was for me? Or did he assume I was like Lizzie, emotional and stubborn?

"You know what he is," he stated again. "You know what he is, and yet you still sit here next to him as though he was someone you could love."

"I do love him," I said.

Without warning, my father stepped forward swiftly and struck my face with his hand. Even Adrian hadn't expected such a reaction or else surely he would have defended me.

I sat in stupor, my hand gingerly caressing my cheek. It didn't even hurt. Not really. And yet, I was stunned. Father had never raised his hand to me, ever. And I had never seen him do it to Lizzie either.

In the blink of an eye, Adrian moved directly in front of my father. His fingers wrapped around my father's throat, lifting him off the ground with one hand. "You dare inflict harm on her?" he asked in a deathly low voice. "Especially in front of me? I never thought you stupid, Reginald."

My father clawed at Adrian's hand, but Adrian didn't budge. Judging by the hold he had on him, it almost seemed as though he put more pressure on my father.

I knew this wasn't Adrian's full strength. If Adrian wanted to, he could crush my father's throat easily. But he wasn't.

"Adrian," I said softly, still dazed by what transpired. I knew my father would be disappointed in me, even angry with my decision. But I'd never considered he would strike out in such a way. "Adrian, please."

"He needs to know he can't touch you in that manner, Hannah," Adrian said without looking at me. "Especially in my presence."

I had nothing else I could say to persuade him to stop, but I tightened my grip on him, hoping he would understand. Adrian's lips curved up, exposing his teeth, as his eyes flashed angrily at my father before slowly setting him down. When my father's feet touched the ground, he loosened his grip on my father's throat but didn't let him go completely.

My father's face was nearly purple. The second he could suck in more air, he did. I had to look away. It didn't sit well with me, to watch my father struggle. Then again if he hadn't treated me so in front of Adrian...

"He needs to realize I care for you," Adrian continued, never taking his eyes off my father.

My father's nostrils flared. "You care for nothing but yourself."

I was surprised my father managed to get as much out of his mouth. The words were garbled and scratchy, and I was sure his throat pinched in pain because of Adrian's touch. But my father would still not listen to reason. It was like he didn't care what he risked by stroking Adrian's ire. If I didn't do anything now, I knew it would only get worse.

"Father," I said, slowly stepping in front of Adrian. Adrian's grip loosened even more, but despite my presence in front of him, Adrian still didn't release his hold on him. "It is the truth."

My father's eyes shifted over to me. This time, there was no mask over his face. It was obvious how he felt. Hurt touched his eyes as if I had been the one to slap him. Guilt pooled out of me, but I couldn't continue to let him use my emotions and control my behavior.

"Adrian does care for me," I continued. "Whether you choose to believe it or not. And I care a great deal for him. And we are engaged to be married."

"No," my father moaned, hanging his head in despair. "No, you can't—"

"I do," I said firmly. "And I'm sorry it's such a disgrace to you, but I won't continue to lie to you. To myself."

My father picked his head up and gave me a long look. "I've tolerated much from Lizzie," he said. "I know it is not fair to hold you to the same expectations since you have always been my good child, the one I could trust. But I must insist you stop seeing him. Break this engagement before... He is dangerous, Hannah. You know what he is—"

"I know what he is, and I still love him," I insisted. "He won't harm me."

"Then you are a fool," my father said. "Even worse than your sister. I can't have you risking my position, risking your sister. If you choose to remain stubborn, if you choose to still marry this monster, you force my hand. Stay with Adrian, Hannah, fine. But you are no longer welcome here. You are to leave, immediately."

CHAPTER TWENTY-FIVE

Hannah

I didn't know what to do with my father's last words. I'd never thought my father would kick me out of my home. After everything Lizzie had done, he'd never once threatened her with something like this. How could he do such a thing now?

Adrian's hand came to rest on my shoulder, snapping me out of my thoughts. As much as I wanted to hurt my father the way I was hurting, I looked up at Adrian and the spell was lifted. There was no point in fighting, I realized. If my father didn't want me here, why should I stay?

I had no idea where I was going to go. I didn't want to assume Adrian would take me in because we had been intimate a couple of times. That wouldn't be fair to him. I could go to my cousins, though my father was certain to tell my uncle, and if my uncle found out, I wouldn't be surprised if his reaction were similar to my father's.

Although, perhaps Brendan would pity me and take me in. I wrinkled my nose at the thought. Even if he would, I realized I didn't want him to do it. Not after the conversation I'd overheard between him and Lizzie.

"Hannah," Adrian murmured. "Come."

I took a deep breath. At least I had some sort of direction, even if I didn't have all the answers. I tilted my chin down in acquiesce and proceeded to follow Adrian out my bedroom door. I held my breath, waiting for my father to call me back, anything that would imply he wanted to take everything back, or he was sorry for even suggesting something so heartless.

I reached the door and my father said nothing. I focused on Adrian's touch, on the next step, and then on the next. I didn't want to look at my father, afraid of what I might find.

The second we stepped outside, I saw my sister standing in the hallway. I knew then she'd sent him into my room because she knew Adrian was here. She'd wanted me to get caught, ruined in the same way she was. She'd taken the perfect opportunity to get back into his good graces and had taken it with no consideration for me. I hated her and how selfish she was. She was my sister, and here she was betraying me.

"How dare you!" I snarled, lunging toward her. A small sense of satisfaction thrilled me when she flinched at my aggressiveness, and at the same moment, Adrian grabbed my wrist and kept me by his side, preventing me from getting any closer to her.

Magick crackled up and down my arm, lifting the hair on my skin.

"You send Father to my room in the middle of the night?" I growled. "I've never, ever betrayed you, Lizzie. You don't think you've given me plenty of cause for concern? But I trusted you."

"Hannah, you don't understand—"

"No," I said. I tugged one of my wrists from Adrian's grasp and thrust my finger in her face. "You don't understand. You never have. You make the assumption you must protect me when the truth is, I've always been able to protect myself. All you see of me is a child. You get to go out and do whatever you want. Father bought you a blacksmith shop. You dress how you like, and live your life how you want. How is that fair? You look at me like I'm some weak thing who can't be trusted with her wants and desires. Now I'm starting to come into who I am, you tell me I'm wrong. You try to parent me, control me, and I am so tired of it all."

Magick shot out of me, causing the paintings hanging on either side of the hallway to crash to the floor. The frames splintered, the art itself forever altered.

Adrian's fingers, still wrapped around my wrist, gave me a gentle squeeze of warning.

"Control it," he murmured.

"I'm trying to protect you," Lizzie said. "If even Brendan comes to me with concerns—" Adrian began to tug me away from my room, from Lizzie, from a life I used to regard as my own. In my distress, the magick pushed against my fingertips, trying to find cracks it might seep out of. I couldn't afford anyone else being privy to it; the result would be disastrous.

With one last glare at Lizzie, I turned away, as Adrian led me away from my room, down the staircase, and into the cold night. I was relieved we'd avoided seeing Diego Pascal or either of his brothers. I was in no mood for Sage's quips, Vibora's lingering stares, or Diego's twisted smile. If ever there was a trigger for my magick, it would have been it.

The second I stepped into the night, I was able to breathe again. I gasped down air, sucking in as much of it as I could. Adrian never released me, even as we made our way toward the gate, not even when we were off the grounds and heading towards the Forest of Legend.

I hesitated. Adrian paused, looking at me. "You're frightened?" he asked. I nodded once, a jerk of my head. Adrian picked me up without warning and rushed through the forest, a swift predator on feet of air as he swept past foliage and branches. I clung to him as tightly as I could, the way I would to a buoy, something to keep myself from going under and drowning. Finally, we made it through the forest and stood by the Black Shore.

He wasn't even out of breath. "I'm going to set you down," he said gently. "Hold on to me until you are steady enough to walk."

I thought I'd be able to stand without assistance, but the second my feet hit the sand, my knees buckled. Adrian's arms wrapped around my waist and held me in place. It wasn't long before my head stopped spinning and I found my footing.

"I've got you," he reminded me, his mouth close to my cheek. His grip on me tightened, and I slowly settled into him, closing my eyes and trying to ignore the burgeoning headache threatening to take over after such a rush. "I've got you."

When I thought I was okay, I pulled away from him slightly, catching his eye and nodding once. I took a tentative step forward, nearly buckling, but I managed to catch myself.

"Let's not do that again any time soon," I said. The corners of his lips quirked up but he said nothing. Instead, he followed me to the old docks that groaned under our weight. I kept glancing down, waiting for them to collapse. Luckily, we reached the end of the dock without incident. We climbed into a small rowboat and Adrian rowed us over to his ship, bobbing softly against the movement of the ocean.

I closed my eyes as exhaustion crept over me like a ghost. By the time we reached his ship, I was nodding away, trying to keep myself conscious. I wanted to sleep. I wanted to crawl between the sheets on Adrian's bed and pretend I hadn't been asked to leave my familial home by my father. Which reminded me...

"Why did you do that?" I asked, tilting my chin up so I could look up at him.

"Do what?" he asked, his shoulders straining as he rowed us closer to the ship.

"Tell my father we're engaged," I said, leaning back. The salt from the sea wafted up and tickled my nose. "I don't understand why you'd do such a thing."

"Are you embarrassed?" he asked.

"Of course not," I said, a frown on my face. "I just don't understand why you would bind yourself to me when it's clear..."

"When what is clear?" he asked. "You silly little fool. How many times must I tell you you're different from the others."

"So...what you told my father is true?" I asked hopefully.

Before he responded, the boat scraped against something, emitting a loud, low groan. I nearly jumped out of my skin—we'd reached Adrian's ship. He reached out and placed a hand on the side, trying to steady the rowboat. I waited as he maneuvered the boat close to the ladder.

Once he had everything right where he wanted, he moved carefully beside me and lifted me up so I could grab the ladder and begin to pull myself up. My arms burned, my muscles straining to lift me. Adrian made no move to help me and I wondered churlishly if he was punishing me for something.

Eventually, I managed to get myself over the banister and counted it as a small victory nonetheless. Of course, Adrian climbed up the ladder with ease, landing on his feet like a panther I'd once seen prowling in the zoo. Every lock of hair was in place; he didn't even appear breathless.

I turned to him, suddenly feeling the cold. I hadn't remembered to grab a coat, and now I was no longer in Adrian's arms, it was easier to start to feel the crisp, cool night.

"You didn't answer my question," I said softly. My voice sounded loud in the quiet of the ship's bow. "Why would you say something like that to my father? About us being engaged?"

"Perhaps because I find it's true," he said. "Even if not in technicality, it is true for me."

"You want to be married to me?" I asked.

He rolled his eyes. "I have already asked to bond with you in a way I haven't asked anyone else," he said with a huff of exasperation. "Why must you question me? Don't you trust my word?"

I hesitated and he sighed loudly, taking a step forward to take my hands in his.

"Use your gift on me. Tell me if I'm lying."

I sucked in a breath. The offer was tempting. And yet, I couldn't bring myself to do such a thing. Trust was about faith. And if I wanted to trust Adrian, I had to believe his word. I wouldn't take advantage of my magick.

"No," I said.

Adrian stared at me for a long while before jerking his chin down in a gesture of acknowledgment. "Come," he said, offering me his hand. "You've had a long night. You must sleep."

"And you?" I asked.

"I must go somewhere, but I won't be gone long."

I nodded. Sleep sounded good—I was ready to collapse into slumber. Hopefully, by morning, we would figure out what to do next.

CHAPTER TWENTY-SIX

Hannah

I didn't sleep well.

Adrian woke me up with a string of kisses up and down my neck. My pulse thrummed against the column of my throat. I was certain Adrian could feel it, even if his attention was on my collarbone, the point of my chin, somewhere else entirely.

"The dawn breaks," he murmured, his lips vibrating against a particularly sensitive part of my skin. Goosebumps trailed my spine and I couldn't suppress a shudder as it tore through my body.

"You're back," I said, my eyes still closed.

"I have returned," he agreed. "But I must sleep. I am…weary."

I opened my eyes, feeling the gentle lull of the waves. I reached overhead, arching my back, and stretching. Adrian's eyes dropped, watching my body carefully, intensely. There was something about his gaze that caused my insides to melt. I wanted nothing more than to pull him on top of me, to shadow myself with his body, to connect with me again and make me forget there was a world outside of this ship that existed, even if was for only a few hours.

However, I kept my desires to myself and pulled him to me instead, so he could rest his head against my shoulder. My fingers slowly began to run through his blond locks. In the content of the moment, my eyes began to droop. I could fall asleep with him like this, I realized. I could pull up the covers, tangle my body with his, and slip into slumber again.

But I had to get up. I wanted to speak to Jessa and see if she might be able to help us regarding the body in Adrian's possession, although I wasn't keen on involving her in this, especially considering how dangerous it was.

"How was your evening?" I asked as I sat up. The sleeve of my gown slid off my shoulder, exposing more skin than I expected. I reached to lift it but Adrian's hand shot out and his fingers curled around mine, preventing me from doing so. "Work, I mean."

"The brothel is nearly reconstructed and better than it was before," he replied. His fingers trailed over the curve of my shoulder. My pelvis tingled with warmth. I had no idea how his touch could affect me so much. It was strange and fascinating and I wanted more of it.

"The girls have no idea what's going on, but Hessie…" His voice trailed off. "She watches me carefully. She knows something is amiss."

"She speaks highly of you," I said slowly. There was an edge to my voice I didn't like, and I dropped my gaze into my lap, bunched sheets tangled around my body.

"Come now." His other hand fingered the underside of my chin before tilting my head up, forcing me to look at him. "You aren't jealous, are you?" There was a smirk on his lips, his eyes soft and amused.

I didn't want to admit it, but I was. I looked down at my hands, fingering the edge of the comforter still tucked around my body, preventing the cold from leaking in. I didn't want to look at him, knowing he would see the truth. Knew he would know exactly how I felt.

Jealousy was such a harsh emotion.

I couldn't outrun it just like I couldn't outrun the truth of my current situation. I needed to accept my lot in life and let the pieces fall where they might

"So what if I am?" I finally asked, turning my head to catch his eyes.

Something glinted in the darkness in his eyes, something that stroked my core in a way only he could.

"What if I don't appreciate other women eyeing you as if you belong to them, like they can do whatever they want to you?" I continued. I let the covers fall farther so I was in nothing but my shift in front of Adrian. The chill clung to my skin, marbling my nipples against the sheer material. "I don't like to think of you being with anyone other than me. I'm sure you wouldn't want to think of me in the throes of passion with any other man—"

I couldn't even finish the sentence before Adrian was on top of me, strong hands pinning me down in the bed. I should be afraid of him. The way his eyes narrowed on me, he was all predator and I was his prey, ensnared by his strength. He wouldn't release me if he didn't want to, and I doubted he wanted to.

"You're mine," he said.

His words filled me with unmatched desire. My mouth went dry. I reached for him, pulling him to me so I could kiss him. My skin buzzed with my magick, and when I touched him, a spark passed between us.

Adrian draped his body across my own, and when he kissed me again, he did so roughly, passionately. His teeth nibbled at my bottom lip until he elicited a cry of pain from me, one he swallowed down with a groan. He clawed at my shift, tugging and pulling the flimsy material until it ripped in a variety of places. His hands roamed my body as if I were the wheel of his ship, needing to steer his fingers to the right place to get me exactly where he wanted me.

I was completely under his command. I tugged at his tunic until it fell open, then pushed it off to fall onto the floor. My hands moved up and down his hard body, loving the way his muscles twitched and spasmed every time I caressed a rather sensitive area.

I grew much bolder than before. Part of me still felt compelled to be embarrassed by my wants, my desire for him, but I quickly pushed those thoughts away. I wanted this and I would have it, without apologies

My lips found the flesh of his neck and I tasted him. As my lips pressed down, he let out a moan, his body stilling under my touch.

I wanted him to live inside of me, wanted to memorize everything about him. I tightened my grip and pulled him even closer to me. His bare chest was hot against my breasts. The scraps of the shift I still wore were nothing, and yet, it was still too much. I didn't want there to be anything between us.

His hands gripped the scraps of my clothing until they fell to the floor, and there was nothing between the two of us. Adrian's desire for me pressed into my thigh, trailing drips of his essence against my skin. I spread myself open until he buried himself inside of me, filling me up with everything he had.

His hands gripped my hips and I automatically shifted underneath him. I was in no mood to play coy, to pretend I cared about how society saw me.

"Tell me," he said in a low voice, fingerprints bruising my sides.

"Please, Adrian," I managed to get out as his teeth scraped the column of my throat.

"Please, what? Say the words," he instructed. There was a brutality to them, and what seemed like a desperate need to hear them. "Tell me."

"Fuck me, Adrian," I said, stumbling over the word despite my confidence. It felt strange to say something so crass, but the groan it caused to rumble in Adrian's throat was well worth it. "Fuck me."

He groaned and pushed harder inside me. I winced at the pain, but as Adrian rocked his body against mine, it quickly subsided into something else.

My hands clutched at him, at his shoulders, the back of the neck, anything that might help tether me to him. I was sure my fingernails would leave marks on him, and the thought of marking him, my passion remaining on his body, spurred me on to rock my hips and tighten my core.

He seemed to feel it too because he grabbed me, arching my back, burying himself up to the hilt.

"Adrian," I managed to get out.

"You're so wet," he growled. I wasn't even sure if he heard me. "So slick and hot and tight."

"For you," I moaned as the nerves inside of me bundled up, each thrust tensing and tightening the muscles in my body. "It's all for you."

He groaned louder and bolts of pleasure struck my core. It was the perfect thing to say. It was exactly what he wanted to hear.

He was touching me in places no one had before, filling me, claiming me as his own. My lips trailed soft kisses up and down the column of his throat as he began to murmur wicked things in my ear: how tight I was, how much I dripped for him, how I was made for him. It was deliriously uncouth and yet strangely romantic. Each word out of his mouth was enough to send me further and further into delirium.

I chased my pleasure and it wasn't long before I let out a low moan at the sensations writhing through my being.

"There you are," he murmured. "It's right there, isn't it? Tell me," he insisted through his moan of pleasure. "I will give you the world. You need only ask for it."

"Make me come, Adrian," I begged. "I need release, I beg of you."

He rutted against me and just like that, I was falling. My nerves bunched up and bloomed, like a flower, and I succumbed to every sensation in my body.

He grunted. "Hannah," he gasped "Hannah, I—"

Following me, he released himself inside of me completely, holding me like I was the only thing keeping him from drowning. And I clung to him just as tightly, afraid to lose this moment, this pleasure.

Slowly, so slowly, my heart resumed its usual pace. Adrian softened inside of me, placing a kiss on my chest, my neck. He pushed himself up, ready to leave me, but I clung to him.

"No," I said. "Don't go."

He kissed my cheek, my chin. "Never," he breathed out.
And I believed him as I settled back into slumber.

CHAPTER TWENTY-SEVEN

Hannah

That night, darkness rolled in sooner than I expected, the moon waning. Adrian had been checking his arrangements and muttered it was getting close to the next shipment of Sirens, and if we didn't solve this soon, Diego Pascal was going to make good on his threats. I agreed. We needed to act now if we were going to stop anything from happening that could result in something that couldn't be undone.

Adrian and I made our way through the forest to meet with Charles, and I kept an eye out for any opposition in the form of one of Thaya's witches, if not Thaya herself. I wasn't exactly sure where the coven was in regards to our current position. The forest was an enigma at night. I almost wished Jessa and I could have done the ceremony on our own during the day, telling Adrian the results once we finished and darkness touched the earth.

But no, of course, Adrian wanted to be present, and I supposed I understood. A branch thwacked my shoulder without warning, earning a gasp of pain from me. I wrinkled my nose in annoyance. Always, something was scratching and clawing at me each time I came to this dreadful place. I sped up to stick closer to Adrian, hoping just being near his tall, muscled frame would protect me from anything else. The sting in my shoulder was abating, at least.

Without warning, Adrian stopped. I ran into his back, causing me to stumble back.

"Is this where…?" I whispered.

"Yes," Adrian said, turning to look at me. He reached out, cupping my cheek in his palm. Suddenly, the sting from the branch didn't hurt as much as it had before. "Thank you. I should have said this before." I blinked. Out of all the things he might say, thanking me was not something I expected from him. The words were coated in affection, and his thumb extended to trace my bottom lip. I reached up and wrapped my fingers around his wrist and sighed in contentment, allowing myself this moment, to wrap myself up in just the two of us. Even if we were in the Forest of Legend, even if this place still spooked me, Adrian had this ability to calm me in a way I couldn't do myself.

"For what?" I finally asked.

"You helped orchestrate this," he said. "Without question. You wanted to help."

"You," I said. "I wanted to help you." There was no way I would go to this much trouble for anyone else, and Adrian knew it.

"Hannah," he said, pulling away from me suddenly. "Whatever we discover tonight…"

"I'll be here," I said. "I won't cower. You can depend on me."

Adrian's gaze dropped to my mouth, and I swallowed as he watched me. "I know you won't," he said softly. "I know I can depend on you, Hannah. You're capable."

His words warmed me more than a coat or a shawl would, even nestled in the Forest of Legend. I wanted to hug him, throw my arms around him and pull him to me. I wanted to capture his lips with mine and kiss him until he struggled to breathe.

His left eyebrow slowly arched up as his irises turned a shade darker, and then another one. He could read me, I realized. He knew exactly what I thought in this moment, and it reflected in his gaze.

"Adrian," I whispered. He said nothing, only caressed my cheek, his obvious affection comforting me. I leaned into his touch, sighing in contentment. Without warning, I leaned forward on my toes and captured his lips.

I slid my tongue in his mouth, and Adrian opened up for me.

As we kissed, warmth coated us. Soft warmth fell on my skin, heating me inside and out. I removed my lips from Adrian's to see flecks of gold touching our skin, slowly falling from the sky like stars.

"What *is* that?" I wondered. I wasn't sure if I was dazed from the kiss or the sight of gold surrounding us in some kind of protective shield.

"Your magick," Adrian said, his voice awed. "Something is changing with your magick. Ever since you left your home, it seems…"

"Freer," I finished, pulling my gaze from my magick to look at him.

"Can you do something with it?" Adrian asked. I lifted one of my hands from Adrian's shoulders and willed the golden light to flow from me and surround Adrian. It was as though I was bathing him in light, my light, like a protective force. My eyes widened as my magick obeyed me, gently flowing toward him and caressing his face the way I did.

His eyebrows shot upward, and there was a moment when it seemed as though he was going to jerk himself away from me. But he stayed still. He let my magick touch him, and the tenseness melted away until his face looked soft.

"You did that," he said in an awed murmur. "You controlled it."

I nodded in delight, watching as more magick floated onto Adrian's face and tickled the tip of his nose before dropping down to the pulse of his throat.

"What does it feel like to you?" I asked. To me, it felt like being a butterfly and fluttering my wings upon the petals of a flower.

"Like what I imagine the sun must feel like," he said. "Warm and soft." He took my hand in his and kissed me slowly before pulling away.

Marcella was right. Controlling my magick had to come from me. More than that, I had to embrace my emotions surrounding my magick. An excited thrum skipped my heart, and I couldn't stop the smile from my face. I wanted to do more, and learn more. If I could do this, what else could I do? I leaned up and kissed Adrian softly.

"I did it," I murmured in disbelief.

He grinned and nodded. "You certainly did."

"Well, isn't this precious," an unfamiliar drawl said from behind us. The second the man interrupted us, my magick completely vanished. "You never told me your cousin was in love with Adrian Blood."

"I haven't seen her in two years," Jessa said, her tone dry. "What do you expect?" I turned so to face Jessa and her companion, who I assumed must be Charles Rochester.

He wasn't as tall as Adrian, but was stocky, packed with muscle. His long hair—a brown color, perhaps a dark auburn—was twisted and tangled into thick locks that ran across his broad shoulders. He wore piratical gear: unwashed tunic and pantaloons, faded blue jacket, cracked leather boots. His face was chiseled, cheekbones high, jawline sharp, with dark gray eyes. He was handsome in a brutal sort of way and hovered protectively over Jessa. I could see why she was drawn to him, why he was the cause of her downfall.

He carried something in his arms. At first, it was difficult to make out what it was in the dark, but as he stepped closer, I realized it was less a something and more a someone, covered by a stained blanket.

"Why do you stare at me so?" Charles asked Jessa. "Do you like looking upon a monster?"

"Don't say such things," Jessa said, holding up her skirts as she stepped carefully over a knotted tree root.

"Why not?" he asked. "It's the truth."

Jessa refrained from saying anything, eyes focused on me. Relief filled her face, though there was confusion too. A litany of questions was reflected in those eyes, but none passed her lips, and I was thankful. Everything that had occurred between me and my family was still too raw to put into words. I wasn't quite ready to speak about it just yet.

"Adrian Blood," the man said with a roguish grin on his face. "Are you going to introduce me to your companion?"

"Fuck off, Charles," Adrian said, surprising me with his candor. His icy gaze fixated on the bundle in Charles's arms. "Is that the body?"

"What else do you think I'd be carrying through the forest?" he drawled, dropping it in a heap on the ground.

Adrian didn't answer. Instead, he stepped toward the body intently. When he reached it, he was careful not to directly touch it. He slowly removed the blanket. I couldn't see what he saw, exactly, but he flinched back, as though he had been slapped.

"Who is it?" I asked, moving to stand next to him, getting a better sight of the poor soul.

The hair was matted. Even with the glow of the moon, I couldn't distinguish the pallor of her skin or the color of her hair. Her eyes burst with blood with irises that stared up to the skies. She appeared to be in a strange in-between phase of Siren and woman, as there were scales on her legs, and fins where her feet should be. No clothes covered her body. I hated my curiosity, staring at her so openly, but I was gruesomely fascinated. Part of me wanted to take the blanket Charles brought her in and cover her, to give the dead woman her dignity and modesty back.

"She's a Siren," he said. "One of mine. Well, she would have been mine."

"How do you know that?" I asked.

Adrian reached out and pointed to her ear. Something was hanging from the shell of her ear. I couldn't make it out but it almost looked like a tag. It reminded me of what farmers did when they cataloged their livestock. My stomach twisted at the comparison. This girl wasn't livestock. She wasn't an animal to keep track of.

"This," he said. "This lets me know she's one of mine. I remove it once she's inside my brothel. Because it's still intact, she never reached me."

"Who do you think would do this to her?" I asked, looking at him.

"I don't know," he said slowly. He pursed his lips, standing straight. He took a step, then another and it wasn't long before he was pacing across the ground, then turning on the balls of his feet and returning. He was deep in thought.

"Where do you think the other one is?" I asked. "You said you were supposed to get two, correct?"

"I don't know," he repeated.

I blew out a breath, crossing my arms over my chest as I tilted my head to the side and regarded the body again. Her face was contorted in pain, and I wished I could wave my hand over it and take it away. As it was, I was helpless.

"Witch," Adrian said, stopping when he reached Jessa. "Can you perform your ritual and trace the magick on the body?"

"How do you know she was killed by magick?" Jessa asked. Even through the darkness, I could see how pale her skin had become. She rivaled the color of the moon, though I wouldn't say she glowed.

"Do you see any other marks on her body indicating otherwise?"

I cut a glare at Adrian, arching one brow. There was no reason for him to be rude. It wasn't as though Jessa knew what to do with a dead body. As it was, I was surprised I could stomach it. I was finding out a lot about myself since meeting my Blood Mage.

"Do your ritual then," Adrian snapped. "We haven't gotten all evening."

Charles grunted some sort of warning but Jessa didn't seem to be offended by Adrian's brusque instruction. She moved over the body and took a deep breath. Placing both hands over the space that encompassed the body, she closed her eyes.

As I watched her, it didn't appear as though she was doing much. The wind tousled my hair, slipping between my dress and my skin like a languid caress. I shivered, stepping closer to Adrian.

And then, a drop of blood appeared from Jessa's nose.

"Jess?" Charles said, concern evident in his deep voice.

Her eyes snapped open and locked onto Adrian. "Siren," she said. She stopped. "I know *she's* a Siren. But the magick that doesn't belong to her, the magick that killed her, belongs to a Siren too."

CHAPTER TWENTY-EIGHT

Adrian

"Jessa, did you say the magick that killed her is *Siren* magick?" Hannah asked, breaking the heavy silence that seemed to envelop our pathetic band of misfits. She nodded toward the body.

"It is," Jessa said with certainty as she wiped the blood from her nose. She shot Charles a look and shook her head imperceptibly. I sensed she was telling him to say nothing about the blood.

"How is this possible?" Charles asked, his voice strangled. "Are you sure?"

"Are you saying I'm mistaken?" Jessa asked with a tinge of aggression.

I didn't need this in-fighting right now. My mind raced with possibilities at what this could mean, and the last thing that was going to help was listening to these two lovers squabble when all they needed was a good fuck to get the tension between them to dissipate.

"Did those words come out of my mouth?" Charles returned. "I simply said Siren magick seems impossible for—"

"It's not," she said flatly. "My magick doesn't lie." She bunched her arms across her chest as though she was protecting herself from something.

"Jessa," Hannah said, taking a step toward her cousin. "Do you know what happened to Jonathan Nyx the night of his Consumption?"

I blinked once, twice. "*That* is what you ask her?" I asked. "We don't have time to concern ourselves with trivialities like Jonathan Nyx, Hannah. We must try to understand how a Siren could raid my business." I focused on her. "You said the magick in the brothel lingered after the raid. And now we have evidence to know the raid itself was Siren instigated."

"Which means it wasn't Lizzie," Hannah murmured thankfully under her breath.

"Lizzie?" Jessa asked in confusion. "Why would you think it's Lizzie?"

Rochester sighed heavily. "Enough of this." He turned to me. "How is it possible Sirens could orchestrate a raid? Do your whores still retain their magick?"

"It's diluted," I said. "At least, that's what I'm told."

"You don't check?" he asked. "You're a fucking fool, Adrian Blood. Do you believe everything Diego Pascal tells you, hmm?"

Jessa looked between the two then pulled her gaze away from us and looked at Hannah. "What's he talking about?" she asked. "What does this have anything to do with Diego Pascal?"

"Must you ladies all ask such irrelevant questions?" I growled at her.

Without warning, Charles was in front of me, fangs extended, nostrils flared. He wasn't as tall as I was, but he was an intimidating presence, even forced to look up at me.

"You will not address her in such a manner," he snarled. "Or I will rip you limb from limb until there's nothing left of you and the birds feed on your carcass."

"Charles," Jessa murmured. Her face was red, even in the darkness. Charles made no indication he'd even heard her. His stare was still fixed on me, and a storm of emotion rolled off him. It was clear to me he cared about her.

"You dare threaten me?" I asked slowly. I didn't appreciate being threatened no matter who was engaging in it.

"If I must," he snapped.

We glared at each other for a few beats until Hannah snorted loudly and we both turned to see her regarding us with a look of amusement.

"I suggest we get back to the problem at hand rather than have you two acting like possessive beasts," she murmured. "Diego Pascal created the Blood Mages."

My eyes snapped to her, and she held my gaze with her steady look, as if to tell me she trusted Jessa and I should too. I wasn't sure it was so easy. After everything Lizzie had done to Hannah, regardless of whether she believed she was protecting her, it didn't mean the betrayal hadn't occurred. How did I know Jessa wouldn't do the same thing with her uncle? If she did, I would make her rue the day. If Hannah was hurt...

I looked back at Charles. Perhaps the two of us shared a better understanding of each other than I initially believed.

"Diego Pascal did what?" Lizzie asked, turning her attention to her cousin.

Hannah proceeded to tell her a short account of what a wretched being Diego Pascal truly was. Jessa's blue eyes continued to widen with each word out of Hannah's mouth. It might have been comical had we been discussing anything else, but as it was, I already felt like we had wasted time figuring out who had raided the brothel, and even then, we didn't know if it had any relevance to the missing Sirens.

By the time Hannah was finished, Charles had finished smoking his rolled tobacco and had his arms folded over his chest.

"So, how did the Sirens orchestrate a raid on your brothel?" he asked.

"I don't know," I said. I didn't like admitting ignorance, but it was the truth.

"You don't know?" Charles's hands dropped to his sides. "Why not?"

"Do you...does your business serve Patrol?" Jessa cleared her throat. I turned to look at her, finding her bouncing from one foot to the other, hands thrust behind her back. It was only then I realized she must be uncomfortable with the business itself.

"I…" My voice trailed off. In truth, I didn't know the specifics of my business. It was something Pepper had always taken care of. Now Pepper was gone, I endeavored to look more into things, but with the missing Sirens, I hadn't had the time. However, I was sure there were records of who supported my establishment in the books.

"The magick…can you tell me specifically who it belongs to?"

"Adrian," Hannah said from beside me. "What are you getting at?"

"Perhaps Jessa can find out some more detail," I said, my gaze on the body resting at Charles's feet. I needed to know exactly who or what type of monster could do something like this.

Jessa closed her eyes, body straining to do as I asked. Charles seemed on edge and I could tell he wanted to stop her, to prevent her from doing anything more. I appreciated she was willing to help, but my patience was running thin. The more time we were out here, the less time we had to find and confront whoever the culprit was. One less day counted down to the fortnight I'd been given, and the remaining days would pass quickly. I needed answers now to protect Hannah, so I could fix this before the consequences were insurmountable.

"It's…it's difficult to ascertain precisely who the magick belongs to." A vein popped in Jessa's forehead. A coat of sweat rested against the exposed part of her chest. "All I can say is it's similar in composition to the magick the body has."

"That doesn't help much." I snarled. The ire in me couldn't be soothed, and in a blink, Charles was in front of me again, baring his fangs.

I roared at him. "Stop your posturing. We don't have time—"

"Adrian!" Hannah snapped. "You'll ruin everything if you don't listen and let her work. I don't think you understand—"

"Your aunt and her coven have been missing for days." I managed to control the tone of my voice but it was still strained.

"I'm not concerned they are going to rush here and discover us. Once your cousin tells me who the magick belongs to, we can finally be done with this."

"That's just it," Jessa whispered. "I can't give you a name. I can tell you about what I sense on the body. A Siren killed her."

"So there you have it," Charles growled. "She's done you your favor."

I was about to retort when Hannah's hand smoothed my chest. Her magick thrummed against me, as she tried to soothe me, to tell me it would be all right. As much as I appreciated the thought, I couldn't be so sure that was the case. I did feel appeased. I blew out a breath through my nose like a frustrated bull but said nothing more.

"I can't explain it," Jessa said slowly, brushing her hair over her shoulders. "Each time I feel magick, I get a feeling, a unique impression from it. While it doesn't exactly tell me *who* the magick is from—I don't get identification from it—I can make out what sort of creature the magick I sense belongs to. As I said, whatever killed her is the same as she is."

I let her words sink in, my eyes going back to the body. The woman's lifeless gaze stared up at the sky, past the tops of the trees, up to the stars.

"Is there anything else you can tell us?" I asked softly. Whether I wanted to admit it or not, Charles was correct. Jessa was doing us a favor, and I didn't want to scare her off. Plus, she was related to Hannah, and she didn't seem to hold any sort of judgment toward her, even though Jessa had seen us kissing earlier. Hannah needed all the family she could get, and I refused to be the cause of any more fractured relations if I could help it.

"The magick is powerful," Jessa said. Despite the chill in the air, her face was still coated with a sheen of sweat. "Unlike any I've ever felt before. I haven't, you know, familiarized myself with Sirens before, of course. This is the first time...but it's potent." She wrinkled her nose. "I'm not sure I'm making any sense."

"You are," I assured her. Hannah gently placed her hand on Jessa's forearm, as though trying to give her cousin some comfort.

Charles stepped over to me, fingers and thumb pressing into his chin, looking deep in thought. "What do you make of all this mess?" he asked in a low and scratchy voice.

I huffed an irritated breath, ready to tell him it was none of his business and I didn't have to explain anything to him. However, deep inside I admitted he had been helpful. And perhaps he'd assist in other ways as well, especially if Jessa was involved.

"Someone murdered her," I said.

Charles's lips thinned. "Why? Who would do such a thing?"

I didn't know. The only thing we were well aware of was the fact another Siren had been responsible for her death. It could have been the girl she was with. It could have been the Siren transporting the bundle. But where was the other girl? Was she dead too, or was she responsible for it?

"The other Siren," Hannah said, as though she could read my mind. "Could it be her?"

"It could," I agreed. My eyes locked with Jessa's. "Unless you noted anything else that might tell us who did it?"

She shook her head. I carefully took in each inflection of her face, of the willow movement of her hair. I needed to know if she was lying to me.

"She doesn't lie," Hannah said softly, and I knew she'd used her magick to check the veracity of Jessa's statement on my behalf. I felt somewhat comforted.

"What exactly is going on?" Jessa asked, looking to Charles for answers.

"Someone is preventing me from getting my shipment of Sirens," I said, answering for him.

"But why?" she queried. "Were they targeting Sirens in general, or your Sirens?"

"We already know it can't be Diego Pascal," Hannah said, her hands curled into fists. "If it was another Siren, why kill their own kind? Why not save them?"

"Unless it's to try to punish Adrian," Charles said, stepping forward. "Perhaps they knew what the punishment would be if Adrian himself didn't receive the shipment."

I looked at the Lost. As much as I didn't want to admit it, he made an interesting point.

"Well?" he continued. "Which Sirens do you know who are also aware of what the repercussions are should you not do as you're instructed to?"

I racked my mind. I doubted the Siren population knew what was going on, especially since they were being sent to me by their own kind. It was the kind of betrayal no one could understand. But someone had to know. There were the messengers…but why kill the Siren? Why not free them? The punishment would be the same if I never received them, to me, at least. Why was murder necessary?

"We need to find out who she is," Hannah said. "The victim. Maybe then we'll get some answers."

"Or I could tell you them myself," a voice said, and before I knew it, we were surrounded by Thaya and her coven of witches.

CHAPTER TWENTY-NINE

Hannah

Something tickled the base of my spine as I watched Thaya and her coven approach us. They didn't head directly for us—some moved left, some moved right.

"What are you doing?" Charles demanded, his eyes narrowed as the witches circled us.

Thaya smirked. She crossed her arms over her chest, staying put as her witches created a circle around us, pinning us inside of it.

This wasn't good.

"Aunt Thaya?" Jessa asked, taking a step toward the woman. I whipped out my hand and caught her wrist. I refused to let her get too close to the woman, afraid of what might happen.

"Jessa, darling," Thaya said, tilting her head to the side and observing her. "So good to see you. You've been keeping in practice with your magick. Tell me, were you able to ascertain who killed her with your powers?" Without even looking at the body, Thaya jutted her chin in the direction of it.

Jessa's eyes widened and she took a step back. She must have stepped on a branch or something because a piece of wood snapped, cracking the silence in two.

"How...?" She looked at me, as though I had any clue how Thaya knew what she did.

I gritted my teeth. Gods, I hoped Lizzie hadn't revealed everything she knew about us all as some sort of good deed to keep in Thaya's good books.

I shrugged. "I don't know how she knows what she does."

"You think me stupid?" Thaya took another step forward, watching Jessa carefully. "As I told Hannah, magick runs through our female line. Your mother possessed magick, as did Hannah's, as do I. Don't you understand? And your sisters all have magick, even if Everly would like to pretend she doesn't."

"No one told you that," Jessa said. "How do you know?"

"I know all," Thaya said carelessly with a wave of a hand. "Just as I know Hannah committed a grave sin by lying with a Blood Mage." Her eyes cut to me and I was rooted in place, unable to look away from her.

"What Hannah does with her body is her choice," Adrian said curtly. He positioned himself in front of me, taking the brunt of Thaya's ire. The second her gaze was off me, I felt as though I could breathe again.

"Not if you're manipulating her to gain something from her," Thaya said, taking a step forward. She didn't seem frightened in the least by Adrian, by what he was or what he could do to her. I wasn't sure if that made her foolish or brave.

"He's not manipulating me," I said, glaring at Thaya and the audacity of the sentiment. "I chose to-to lie with him. I choose to be with him. You can't stop me."

"I can and I will," Thaya said, eyes narrowed. "Your magick is too precious to use on the likes of him." She tilted her head to the side, and then looked back at Jessa. "As is yours, niece. I took matters into my own hands with Charles Rochester. He ruined you, ruined your reputation, and in your heartache, your magick flourished."

Jessa raised her palm to her forehead. "What...what are you saying?" she asked. "What did you do?"

"He ruined you, Jessa," Thaya said. "He ruined you. He was going to leave you forever—"

"No," Charles contended. "I was going to marry her."

"You?" Thaya spat. She finally deigned to give Charles her attention. "You are nothing, a speck of sand on a beach. You are a Pyrate. The only thing you'll marry eventually is a noose."

Jessa's head snapped to her left, as though she had been slapped. It was as though she couldn't quite believe Charles was what he was still, and each reminder was another painful blow she couldn't defend herself against.

"I found him on his ship," Thaya continued, her eyes lighting up with pure delight. "He knew who I was, my relation to you, and immediately thought something had happened to you. I took advantage of his assumption and I brought him to a hoard of Blood Mages—hungry, desperate to feed on anything that wasn't livestock."

"Stop it," Jessa said. "Stop lying."

I decided now was as good as any to see if Thaya was lying. I closed my eyes. Dangerous but I had to do it. I left myself vulnerable. However, it was important to decipher if Thaya was someone who could be trusted. Lizzie seemed to trust her wholeheartedly while something inside me resisted the very notion of doing so. I didn't know who to listen to anymore. I doubted myself because I had been wrong before—about Adrian, my father, Lizzie herself. What if I was wrong again and Thaya just wanted to help?

I let my magick swarm my aunt, let it touch her words, gliding over them, tasting them, feeling them. Was Charles truly a Blood Mage? I wanted to ask Adrian, but it wasn't his secret to tell.

True. She was telling the truth. My eyes snapped open. "Jessa," I said in a low voice.

Somehow, she heard me. Her head snapped in my direction. She must have recognized the look on my face because her face paled and she keeled over like someone had hit her in the gut. Her hands clasped her knees as her head hung down, and she gasped for air.

"Jessa," Charles said, tentatively coming to stand next to her. "I'm so sorry."

"I speak the truth," Thaya said. She began to move in my direction, hands on her hips. Her attention was on me now, even though she addressed Jessa. "And you were able to confirm it with your magick. A talent indeed."

I shifted. I didn't like the way she eyed me like I was a scrap of meat and she was a stray dog, intent on taking advantage of what I could offer her. I took a step back but there was nowhere for me to go. Adrian slid in front of me, offering what protection he could. I appreciated the sentiment, even though something inside me told me it didn't matter what he did, Thaya was going to get to me in any way she knew how.

"I can help you," she said. "I know you long to control your magick. I can scent your fear of it, even from where I stand. But you don't have to be afraid, niece."

"You just told Jessa you turned her lover into a Blood Mage," I remarked. "How could I not be afraid of you?"

"Charles Rochester is an unruly distraction who desecrated Jessa whenever he saw fit and left her to fend for herself," Thaya all but spat. Her fingers balled at her sides, tension shaking her arms. "He's a coward. He ruined her without a thought to the consequences Jessa now faces. She fell out of favor with her father and no man will touch her."

"I'm sure you're pleased about that," I said before I could stop myself.

"And what does that mean?" Thaya asked, furrowing her brows while taking a step closer.

"Lizzie fell out of favor with my father as well, something you took advantage of," I said. The more I spoke, the more my confidence grew. Something inside me told me I was right about this, I was right about her. I knew I had Adrian to support me, protect me. I had Jessa and even Charles. I wasn't alone. "She's looking for approval from someone, anyone. You probably hoped for the same thing with Jessa, especially knowing what sort of magick she has, what she can discover. Did you have anything to do with Adrian not receiving his shipment, Aunt Thaya? We know a Siren wound up killing the girl, but did you orchestrate it?"

There was a heavy silence, and something twisted and knotted my stomach. The wind picked up, whistling overhead as it tugged and pulled at the trees. The leaves whispered their warnings, something I should have taken more heed to. Perhaps I had gone too far. Perhaps I spoke about something I didn't know the truth to. I didn't have actual proof Thaya was behind any of it, just an assumption, but something inside felt right about it, and that was what mattered.

"There is much you don't know, little girl," Thaya said. "You believe you're in love with that thing, but Adrian Blood is a mere tool used by the wealthy to orchestrate a war between two kingdoms—not even Cardonia, but Ankura, a tiny little port town, will fall to its knees the second the Sirens come for us. The Legacies have already deemed Ankura worth sacrificing. They arranged for this; both kingdoms did. And the Sirens must suffer for it. But what Adrian Blood doesn't know, what the Pascals and the Legacies don't know, is the Sirens plan to use this as a reason to go to war fully, completely, to take over Cardonia. They plan to kill the Blood Mages. And why wouldn't they? This is the perfect excuse to get rid of them all."

"You lie," Adrian roared, his face paler than usual.

"Do I?" She turned to me, hands on her hips, a smirk on her face. "Tell him, Hannah. Use your magick on me and tell him if I'm lying."

I wanted to think this was some sort of trick, but I highly doubted she'd be as smug as she was right now if that were the case. I took in a breath and closed my eyes. I leaned into her words, trying to feel out the lie. Lies stuck out, like skin near a nailbed, something that didn't belong. I ran over the words once, twice, just to be sure.

I opened my eyes, locked them with Adrian's, and slowly nodded my head. "She does not lie either."

"See?" Thaya said gleefully. "A tool. A pawn. You are insignificant in the grand scheme of things."

"What do you want?" I snapped. I wouldn't let her sit here and insult Adrian in front of me.

"I want what you want, Hannah," Thaya said. "I want you to thrive. I want you to learn of your magick, understand it. I want you to empower yourself so you don't easily fall for the tricks and manipulation of those around you, whether Blood Mage or simply a man in power. I want the world at your feet."

I let her words sink in, my breathing heavy. I glanced at Adrian, but he wouldn't even look at me. His gaze was fixed on Thaya, shoulders rigid, arms poised at his sides like he wasn't sure what her next move would be.

"I want the same for Jessa," she continued. "For all of my nieces. This is what your mothers wanted for you as well, but they were taken from us before they had the chance to do it themselves. The responsibility now falls to me. And it is one I'm glad to accept. Lizzie has already exceeded my expectations, and I know you both will do the same."

"But what if we don't want that?" Jessa asked. "I…I appreciate my magick, but it's still a ticking grandfather clock. Things are still building up until they reach a breaking point where I could be on the pyre, waiting to go up in flames the way Jonathan Nyx did. It isn't worth the risk."

"Your magick is always worth the risk," Thaya snapped, leaning forward and glaring. "Because it is part of you, and *you* are worth the risk. Don't you understand ?"

"And you can help us?" Jessa asked, doubt coating her words.

"I can make you more powerful than you have ever imagined," my aunt said with the utmost certainty.

"What if we don't want that?" I asked before I could stop myself.

"What do you mean?" Thaya's brows drew together. She was perplexed about my words, though I didn't understand why. I glanced around at the other witches who had caged us in; they had the same looks on their faces, as though the mere notion I didn't want such power was akin to blasphemy.

"I don't need to be powerful," I said. "I don't want it, especially not with the way you seek to give it."

"Then I say you're naive, niece," Thaya sneered. "You trollop around for Adrian, not caring about your reputation, not looking to the future to understand the consequences of your actions. Each day you refuse to learn of your magick is another day wasted. I want to give you the tools to empower yourself while all you care about is being wrapped up in a Blood Mage who can't pledge his heart to you. He doesn't have one, Hannah. And what happens if you're right? If he does love you? And you grow old and he doesn't. Will he turn you into what he is? What then? Or had you even considered such a situation?"

The truth was, I hadn't considered such a thing. I blew out a breath. "Even so," I said, "that doesn't mean I will approve of your educational tactics. You wish to harm Adrian, Charles, whatever Blood Mage you can because you see them all as a threat. If that's your idea of power..." I shook my head. "I don't want it."

There was a moment of stunned silence. None of the witches knew how to react. Then, my aunt took a step closer to me. "Unfortunately for you, Hannah, you don't get a choice in the matter. If you won't come freely, we will just have to use force."

She gestured imperiously to her coven. "Take them."

CHAPTER THIRTY

Hannah

Thaya and her witches weren't going to let us leave and they were here to fight. Whether they wanted the body, the two Blood Mages, or me and Jessa, I didn't know. Perhaps they wanted everything.

There was no time for me to waste and I was forced to raise my hands and defend myself, as was Jessa. Charles and Adrian were already surrounded, which meant Jessa and I would be counted on to fight for ourselves, without any assistance.

Magick slid out of my hands as I raised them against a witch with dark skin and gray eyes. Her magick reminded me of angled, long spider legs, searching and stretching. A tendril brushed my cheek and my skin sizzled beneath it. I yanked my head back and aimed my magick at her. Blue tendrils came spilling out of me, writhing uncontrollably. It wasn't exactly what I had in mind, but I couldn't control myself the way these witches did.

The witch easily dodged my magick, skipping to the side and throwing her arm out to fire more winnowy magick at me.

I fell back, landing on my backside. My tailbone cracked and I bit my bottom lip to keep myself from grunting in pain. I couldn't give them the satisfaction of knowing they'd hurt me. Not when Jessa was holding her own, when they were actively trying to take down Charles and Adrian. For some reason, they were going easier on me.

"Come on," I shouted, standing up. I ignored the pain in my backside as I shifted my weight. "Come on!"

My frustration caused even more of my magick to spill out. It rushed toward my target, and this time she couldn't escape. My magick consumed her, causing her to fall, to scream and writhe in pain.

I watched her, part of me delighted in seeing her incapacitated because of me. The only time before I'd been able to use my magick was when Adrian had been kidnapped by Pepper when she was going to kill him.

Now, it seemed I could control it more and it came to me when I called it. The problem was, I was concerned there was too much, and it was difficult to focus it in a specific direction. It could hit in front of me, but what if she'd darted away? What if the magick was sluggish and unable to keep up with her? I needed to refine it so it obeyed me in all aspects. It wouldn't be long before I was depleted and this attack had only just begun.

Something clipped my shoulder and pain struck as the skin opened up. Blood seeped into the thin material of the dress I wore, and I stumbled forward. My eyes stung with tears and I whirled around, only to see another witch, golden tendrils dancing around her fingers, waiting.

"We don't wish to harm you, Hannah," she said. This time, I used my other magick to decipher the truth from her words. I didn't care whether it was right or wrong. After everything, I knew I needed to protect myself in whatever way I could, and that meant using the resources I had at my fingertips to bring the truth to me.

I leaned into the instincts, into the words. They were coated with sugar, something this witch meant but only emphasized with a false sense of warmth. She wanted me to trust her so she could take advantage.

"Perhaps not," I said, drawing my magick out in front of me, a horizontal glow trailing after the direction of my fingers. "But that doesn't mean you don't have an idea of what you want from me. Tell me, what is it?"

She shot a string of magick spears at me. I took my magick and dodged once, twice. The third sliced into my shoulder, and I couldn't help giving a strangled cry. The magick burned, sizzling my skin. I wasn't even sure if I was bleeding or if it was merely my skin, distorted and charcoaled now.

It didn't matter. I took the pain, the anger, the confusion, and infused my magick with those emotions. It grew and increased in the palms of my hands. When I threw it at her, she didn't have a chance to create a shield. It swallowed her whole, her scream the only thing left of her for a heartbeat or two. After a moment, my magick faded, and the witch dropped into a heap on the floor. I wanted to go check on her, fearing I'd killed her, but I couldn't let myself be distracted.

I whirled around, looking for Adrian, wanting to ensure he was still all right. There were three witches at his feet, blood oozing out of their bodies. He moved fast and fluid, like running water. I didn't know if they were dead or not, but if they were, I couldn't fault him for doing what he thought he had to, to protect himself, or me. I didn't know these witches, and while I didn't want them to perish, I would rather see them gone than Adrian or Jessa or even Charles. Perhaps that made me selfish. Perhaps the Five Gods would punish me accordingly, and perhaps I deserved it.

But I would do everything I could to protect those I cared about…those I loved.

I sucked in a shaky breath. Then, without warning, something struck me from behind, propelling me forward. I landed on the hard dirt, my knees screaming in protest. I clenched my teeth, hoping to drown out the shout of both surprise and pain.

I tried to push myself up but was clipped by another shot of magick, straight to my other shoulder blade. I fell forward again.

"Stubborn wench," a voice said. "Stay down."

It was the smart thing to do. But I couldn't bring myself to just lie there when everyone else was still fighting. I placed my palms on the dirt and, ignoring the strain in my arms, and the sting in my back, I pushed myself up to my knees.

Tears blurred my vision. I hurt too much to pretend it didn't affect me. Grunting with the exertion, I finally stood, wiping my palms together. Little pieces of dirt fell to the ground, along with small drops of blood.

There are too many witches, all with more knowledge and experience than me.

Doubt assailed me. I was nothing compared to them. I doubted Jessa could compare to them as well. We didn't belong to the coven, didn't have someone training us on how to use our magick.

Another shot of magick snapped toward me. I lifted my hand, envisioning a gold shield around my body. The magick hit the shield and bounced off, disappearing as it fell to the ground and dispersed.

Unfortunately for me, the shield itself was exhausting to hold. It flickered once, twice, before going out completely. I sucked in a breath. This wasn't going to end well for us. There had to be something I could do.

A grunt pierced the air. There seemed to be a lot of noises emitted by someone or something during this fight, filled with pain and anger and sadness. But Adrian had been silent through it all—until now.

I whirled around, not caring I gave my opponent my back. I had to see what was going on with Adrian. I had to ensure he was all right. I moved as quickly as my feet could carry me. It wasn't far, not when my body ached. Not when outside magick still thrummed through my body with static. I saw Adrian immediately. He was on his back, staring up at the sky. Something must have happened, something keeping him in place because he would surely have already gotten up if he had any choice in the matter.

"Adrian?" I asked. I stumbled as if my feet had forgotten how to take me from one point to the next. I nearly fell forward, but I caught myself on the grass, the dew moistening my palms and staining my dress. I didn't care I was getting wet—I had to see if he was all right.

Adrian blinked once as I leaned over him. Something about his taut cheeks and strained jaw told me he was in pain even though I couldn't see what was causing him to feel this way.

"Are you hurt?" I asked, trying to keep the tremble from my voice. "Tell me, what ails you?"

He opened his mouth, but nothing came out. I clutched at his hand, tears blurring my vision. I tried to blink them away. I was supposed to be strong. Emotions took hold of my body freely, touching every part of my body. Magick seeped out of me, just like it had before when we had kissed not an hour ago. Golden light coiled around Adrian's body and I wasn't sure if I was healing him or if I was protecting him from another attack.

"Why must you waste your magick on him?" Thaya asked scathingly. Something struck Adrian then, slicing through my magick with ease and hitting his chest.

He released a grunt, grinding his head deeper in the grass. I gasped at the sight of his suffering.

No. They would not do this to him.

I tightened my fists, trying to pour more of myself into protecting him and me. I needed my magick to be strong. I needed to ensure nothing could get Adrian, even if it left me vulnerable.

"Tell me, niece," Thaya said. "I want to understand you."

"I love him," I said. I didn't care what she thought; it was the truth. It was an answer I knew most would roll their eyes at, most wouldn't believe. To sacrifice the life I had, to give up my family, my status, my privilege, all because I wanted to be with Adrian was daft. I knew this. And yet, I would make the choice over and over again.

"I can't sit and let you throw your life away for some monster who doesn't appreciate you," Thaya said, stepping closer. I could see the hem of her dress wet with dew, the way the grass and the dirt clung to the bottom of her boots. "He will never love you in return."

"That's a lie," I said. "He loves me. Whether you choose to believe it or not doesn't matter. I believe it."

"You would give up your magick—"

"How would I give up my magick?" I demanded to know. I wanted to keep her talking. At least this way, she wasn't throwing magick at Adrian. Hopefully, it gave him enough time to heal. "My love for Adrian doesn't need to mean I'm sacrificing myself in the process. I can have both. It is possible."

"What do you know of love?" Thaya asked. "Of magick?"

Without warning, she flung more magick at Adrian. I darted in front of it without thinking. It struck my chest, between my breasts, pushing me back. I fell past Adrian in a heap on the grass. I was also now coated with dew and dirt. Leaves tangled themselves in my hair, twigs pressed into my back. But the pain was the only thing I detected. It pierced my very essence, ripping its way inside of me, twisting and tangling itself around my heart until breathing wasn't an option. I couldn't even draw in breath from my nostrils.

I'm going to die.

I clawed at my chest, trying to send my magick inside of me, to fight this outside force, but nothing came out of my fingertips. Sparks fizzled and died.

"Hannah." Was that Thaya's voice calling for me? The sound was muffled; it was hard to distinguish it. "I implore you to stop this. I don't wish to harm you further. It would be a waste of magick. Please."

"No, I…" I swallowed, and suddenly, whatever was in me was gone in a flash. Suddenly, I could breathe again. I filled my lungs with as much air as I could, like breaking the surface of the water after believing drowning was imminent. "I can't let you harm Adrian. I can't…I won't."

Thaya's anger flared in her eyes.

"I will do whatever it is you want from me," I continued, still struggling to breathe. My throat was raw, my voice scratchy. "Just leave Adrian alone."

"I can't, Hannah," Thaya said. "For too long, the magicked have been persecuted. After my sisters both disappeared, I knew I had to do something. I won't let our kind be persecuted any longer, do you understand?"

"Adrian doesn't wish to persecute us," I pointed out. Slowly, I eased myself up. Pain corded my muscles, but it was a numbing sensation rather than something that cut deep. "Neither does Charles. Most Blood Mages aren't even aware we exist. They too long to be left alone."

"They feed on humans to sustain life," Thaya snapped. "It goes against the natural order." She waited until I pulled myself back up into a standing position. "There is so much for you to learn…" She glanced at Jessa before looking back at me. "How about we engage in a bargain?"

"No," Charles said gruffly. He was on the floor, one of the witches with her foot on his chest. Magick must be keeping him down because there was no way Charles was so weak. "Don't do it, Jessa. She's a snake. She will—"

"What sort of bargain?" I asked.

"You come with us," Thaya said slowly, "and I'll promise you your Blood Mage lives. We won't hurt him. Not at all."

"You won't steal away his Sirens?" I asked firmly.

"Hannah," Adrian said, groaning. "Do not—"

"If Diego Pascal wants to kill him, he can find his own reason to do so," Thaya stated.

I nodded. "All right," I said. "I'll agree. But there's one other thing I want in return."

Thaya smirked. "Name it."

"I want the name of the Siren who killed Adrian's shipment," I said. "The one you're working with."

"Done." She stuck out her hand, magick tendrils dancing between her fingers. "Do we have an accord?"

I hesitated, staring. I knew she was going to bind me to this. Unfortunately, I didn't have a choice.

"Yes." I stuck my hand in hers, merging my magick with hers.

"The Siren's name you're looking for is Hessie," she said. Then she released my hand, magick still sparking at my fingertips.

I was bound to her and there was nothing I could do about it.

OTHER BOOKS IN THE SERIES

Sea & Ash

ABOUT THE AUTHOR

USA Today Bestselling Author Isadora Brown is a Disney villain addict, a sucker for Persephone and Hades retellings, and a lover of all things dark and forbidden. She believes in happily ever afters, a mystery that leaves readers guessing until the last minute, and stubborn characters set out to achieve their dreams even if no one else thinks they will.

A Southern California girl at heart, Isadora currently resides in a small lake town in Michigan with her husband, four children, and her plethora of fur-babies.

Stay in touch by subscribing to her VIP newsletter:
https://view.flodesk.com/pages/5ec2d2d61bb82200264a1e7b

CONNECT WITH ISADORA
IG: @authorisadorabrown
FB: /authorisadorabrown
BookBub: /authors/isadora-brown

www.BOROUGHSPUBLISHINGGROUP.com

If you enjoyed this book, please write a review. Our authors appreciate the feedback, and it helps future readers find books they love. We welcome your comments and invite you to send them to info@boroughspublishinggroup.com.

Follow us on TicTok and Instagram, and be sure to sign up for our newsletter for surprises and new releases from your favorite authors.

Are you an aspiring writer? Check out www.boroughspublishinggroup.com/submit and see if we can help you make your dreams come true.

Love podcasts? Enjoy ours at www.boroughspublishinggroup.com/podcast

www.ingramcontent.com/pod-product-compliance
Lightning Source LLC
Chambersburg PA
CBHW031333170626
46807CB00002B/679